I wish the reader to take notice that in the writing of [this book] I have made myself a recreation of a recreation; and that it might prove so to him, and not read dull and tediously, I have in several places mixed, not any scurrility, but some innocent, harmless mirth; of which, if thou be a severe, sour-complexioned man, then I here disallow thee to be a competent judge; for divines say there are offenses given, and offenses not given but taken.

– **Izaak Walton,** *The Complete Angler*

Bickerstaff ventured to tell the Town, that they were a parcel of Fops, Fools, and vain Cocquets; but in such a manner, as even pleased them, and made them more than half enclined to believe that he spoke Truth.

– **John Gay,** *The Present State of Wit*

I hope no Reader imagines me so weak to stand up in the Defence of **real** *Christianity, such as used in Primitive Times (if we may believe the Authors of those Ages) to have an Influence upon Men's Belief and Actions: To offer at the restoring of That would indeed be a wild Project; It would be to dig up Foundations, to destroy at one Blow all the Wit, and half of the Learning of the Kingdom; to break the entire Frame and Constitution of Things.*

– **Jonathan Swift,** "An Argument against the Abolishing of Christianity in England"

THE

Devil's

DIC•TION•AR•Y OF THE CHRISTIAN CHURCH

2ND EDITION

DONALD T. WILLIAMS, PhD

WITH AN APPENDIX BY

MARK GERL

STONE TOWER PRESS

The Devil's Dictionary of the Christian Church
2nd Edition

Stone Tower Press
7 Ellen Rd.
Middletown, RI 02842
stonetowerpress.com

ISBN: 979-8-9940926-8-2

Formatting and cover design by Amy Cole, JPL Design Solutions

Printed in the United States of America

TABLE OF CONTENTS

INTRODUCTION:

In his infamous *The Devil's Dictionary*, early twentieth-century journalist Ambrose Bierce gave us one of the great masterpieces of curmudgeonry in the history of literature. His delightfully wicked definitions and sprightly, mischievous verses poke gaping holes in the bubbles of human vanity and pretension. Thus, *admiration* is "Our polite recognition of another's resemblance to ourselves." A *bigot* is "One who is obstinately and zealously attached to an opinion that you do not entertain." A *conservative* is "A statesman who is enamored of existing evils, as distinguished from the Liberal, who wishes to replace them with others." *Erudition* is "Dust shaken out of a book into an empty skull." But that is enough to go on with. I do not wish to deprive you of the pleasure of making Bierce's acquaintance yourself. It is sufficient just to whet your appetite.

Well. I had the good fortune to have been perusing Bierce the same day that I had occasion to consult that marvelous and serious reference work, *The Oxford Dictionary of the Christian Church*. That was a confluence of events which my more refined and intelligent readers will consider fortunate, though to many sour, narrow, and humorless souls it will no doubt appear regrettable. For I was struck with a sudden inspiration, rife with potential for the enlightenment and edification of humankind.

It seemed to me that, there being no organism with a more high, noble, and serious purpose than the Church of our Lord Jesus Christ, there was therefore no organism more desperately in need of the ability to laugh at its own foibles. For such is the weakness of human nature—even of redeemed and somewhat sanctified human nature—that importance bleeds over into self-importance most subtly and dangerously. And self-importance leads to self-ignorance, and self-ignorance opens the door to immeasurable folly. Hence the depressing form that normality takes in the Church in most ages, especially, it seems, our own. And hence, too, the title of this work. This is, as it were, a Screwtapian devil looking at the Church through the lens of diabolical wishful thinking and receiving way too much help from the Church herself to aid him in maintaining his illusions. When Christ returns, she will be seen in a different light. But, sadly, if History is any guide, not until then.

Let there then be no misunderstanding (yeah, right!). If some people do not get offended by this work, it will have failed in its purpose. But I have no wish to give *unnecessary* offense. If you, gentle reader, are told that, for example, *counseling* is a ministry designed to provide fools and incompetents with psychological jargon they can use to excuse their irresponsibility and misbehavior, you should not conclude that the author thinks that it is always so, or that he necessarily thinks that you are thus. Some of his best friends are counselors—it is a role he has taken himself, hopefully without incarnating his definition. Some of his best friends have been counselees. And *some* of those friends have been stellar exceptions to his definition, people who have given and received real spiritual wisdom and psychological help. Remember: the definition is what the Devil *wishes* were true, period, and which is in fact true all too often. So, don't get offended; just be one of the Exceptions.

The Dictionary covers not only the Church and her history, divisions, movements, institutions, ministries, personalities, and theology proper (or improper as the case may be), but also movements in philosophy, general culture, etc., which affect her ministry, such as Modernism, Post-Modernism, and Post-Post-Modernism. It was going to cover Post-Post-Post-Modernism, but one has to draw the line somewhere. Every effort has been made to be an equal-opportunity stepper-on of toes. The author believes and hopes that those attached to the feet of his own tradition will be smarting more than anyone else's. The only feet he has encountered (most definitely including his own) that were not pointedly composed of clay bore some rather peculiar scars.

Women and minorities are encouraged to buy this book (including copies for all their friends and relatives). No animals were harmed in the making of this Dictionary, though a certain chihuahua did give the author some rather strange, puzzled looks. But, then, she is not the only one who does that.

Ever since the days of Swift, history has recorded that satirists tend to be serious people whose acerbic wit is a defense mechanism to help them in the necessary task of beating off despair. Such is the case with me. I love the Church for the sake of her Lord, and my life is dedicated to serving her. (I hope my recent book *Ninety-Five Theses for a New Reformation: A Roadmap for Post-Evangelical Christianity*, Semper Reformanda Publications, 2021, sufficiently supports that claim.) Let no one draw any other conclusion from the seeming snideness of what follows here. For my experience in writing these definitions has been one of profound sadness at how often I realized that, while the effect I had aimed at was biting humor, the resulting portrait seemed not so much a caricature as the simple and unadorned truth. Yet in that very sadness lie paradoxically the seeds of hope. Our Lord is great enough to use even this Church; He is even great enough to love her. He is even gracious enough to love you and me.

God has a very healthy sense of humor. This I take to be self evident from the fact that He created the platypus and the fact that He puts up with you and me. But for some reason, a large number of His children seem to lack this basic bit of equipment, necessary for sanity in a fallen world. Therefore, the author, the Irreverend Dr. Donald T. Williams, hereby disavows all responsibility for the composition of this excellent work. He did not write it, and you cannot prove that he did.

Williams did write the poems in *Stars through the Clouds: The Collected Poetry of Donald T. Williams*, 2nd edition (Lantern Hollow Press, 2020), some of which were pirated for inclusion in this

Dictionary; but he cannot be blamed for that. In their original context they were simple expressions of goodness, truth, and beauty, and not satirical or sarcastic *at all*.

PREFACE TO THE SECOND EDITION

In the almost two decades since *The Devil's Dictionary of the Christian Faith* was first published, its Author, whether due to the decadence of the age or to sheer stubbornness on his own part, has not been moved to take back a single Definition. Indeed, the perversity either of the age or of his heart (or both) has caused him to add about forty new words which, despite the innocence of the church and its manifest daily increase in *Piety* (q.v.), *Spirituality* (q.v.), and *Sanctification* (q.v.), seem to call for clarification.

With this book having already been before the public for almost twenty years, there was every reasonable expectation that Renaissance, Reformation, and Revival, yea, a third Great Awakening, should have resulted. That these fruits did not follow from the book's first publication can only be attributed to the negligence of the Booksellers, who somehow failed to convince the reading public that it existed. Wait ... that the book existed or that the reading public existed? Oh, never mind.

Why the anonymous Author of this regrettable work (who is most certainly *not* Donald T. Williams, PhD) wishes to Disturb the Slumber of the Saints with the Prick of the Needle of Satire once again is unclear. Based on the sales of the first edition, it cannot be for pecuniary gain. Nevertheless, you should purchase multiple copies of the second edition for all your friends, relatives, acquaintances, and enemies, not to mention passing strangers, plus several additional copies just in case you ever need them. If you buy at least ten more copies than you can afford, paying cash, of course, you are guaranteed to receive a tenfold Blessing of extravagant Health and Wealth in this life, and in the life to come, well, you will just have to wait and see.

THE DEVIL'S DICTIONARY OF THE CHRISTIAN CHURCH

"Slanders, sir; for the satyrical rogue says here..."
—Hamlet

A

Abolition of the Slave Trade (n.): The "pretty pass" which Lord Melborne rightly feared things in Britain would come to if religion were allowed to interfere with public life.

Abomination (n.): Something really bad, like going to movies, listening to popular music, thinking, or playing sports on the Sabbath.

Abstinence (n.): Giving up pleasure in exchange for an augmentation of pride. *Protestants* (q.v.) are ranked on a scale from Fundamentalist to Evangelical to Neo-Orthodox to Liberal to Radical based on how favorable an exchange they think this is.

The Fundamentalist's Creed

"Knowing that sharp deprivation
Is the most assured path to salvation,
  Though it gives me great pain,
  I vow to abstain
From all pleasures save argumentation."

Accompaniment (n.): The plinking, droning, and/or twanging which serves to distract attention from the *Congregation's* (q.v.) failure to sing the *Hymns* (q.v.) or the *Choir's* (q.v.) or Soloist's insistence on singing the *Anthems* (q.v.) or *Special Music* (q.v.).

Accompanist (n.): One who provides *Accompaniment* (q.v.); the musician who does most of the work for none of the glory.

"An Account of Things Accomplished": An Exposition of the Gospel according to Luke. Franklin, NC: Christicommunity Press, 2024 (n.): As if it were not bad enough that people keep reading the Bible (or, at least, buying copies of it), now that pestiferous pastor and scholar *Donald T, Williams, PhD* (q.v.) has had the audacity to try to explain it. No Christian looking for sound exposition relating the ancient text to the needs of the contemporary church should have anything at all to do with this book.

Adduce (v., t.): To cite in support of; cf. *Prooftext.*

> To say that his logic was loose
> In the texts that he chose to adduce
> Would be far too kind;
> What came out of his mind
> Was closer to audience abuse!

Administration (n.): Those officers in the *Church, Denominational Home Office, Bible College*, or *Christian College* (q.v.) whose function is to rationalize the failure of the institution to pay a living wage, achieve its mission, or even pursue its goals.

> What form of madness or inebriation
> Comes with the mantle of Administration
> To send the Conscience into hibernation
> And make the oral cavity
> Descend into depravity
> With no defense against prevarication?

Agnostic (n.): One who thinks he has better sense than to get started in debates about religion. With most of the potential debating partners available, he is right.

Agnosticism (n.): The doctrine that either we do not or cannot know that God exists, so we might as well live as if He does not.

Aisle (n.): A space that separates rows of *Pews* (q.v.); a crucial element in Protestant church architecture, as it facilitates the three most important parts of the service: the *Offering* (q.v.), the *Altar Call* (q.v.), and the stampede for the exit after the *Benediction* (q.v.).

Allegorical (adj.): Pertaining to an alternative method of interpretation which, instead of ignoring the *Context* (q.v.), ignores the words themselves.

Alliteration (n.): The repetition of initial consonant sounds to create the illusion of a planned sequence of headings in the *Sermon* (q.v.); Apt Alliteration's Artful Aid; Purposefully, Perniciously, and Pointedly to Pick a Pulchritudinous Progression of Perfectly Putrid P's to Punctuate in Passing one's Paltry Passel of Potentially Perverse, Patently Pusillanimous, and Possibly Pestiferous Points? Precisely.

Mad method of much ostentation,
Sweet sounding sermonic sensation:
    To madden the Muse
    And boldly abuse
The apt art of alliteration.

Altar (n.): In ancient Judaism, a pile of stones where animals were sacrificed; in Roman Catholicism, a piece of furniture near the Transept where wafers are sacrificed; in Fundamentalism, the steps leading up to the platform where the reason of the members is sacrificed; in Pentecostalism, a similar location where their sanity is sacrificed; in Evangelicalism, that region of the soul off from which living sacrifices are accustomed to crawl.

Altar Call (n.): A protracted period (averaging anywhere from ten to thirty minutes in duration) which begins only after the service has already gone overtime; that moment, in the liturgy of those churches which have neither liturgy nor altars, when the *Preacher* (q.v.) attempts to validate his ministry through emotional manipulation; a contest of wills in which it is seen how many times through "Just as I Am," "Lord, I'm Coming Home," or "Softly and Tenderly, Jesus is Calling" the congregation can tolerate.

Such weeping and wailing and curses!
What horrible fates or reverses
    Could cause such a thing?
    "With our heads bowed, let's sing,
Softly now, one more time, all the verses."

"Amazing Grace" (n.): The most popular *Hymn* (q.v.) ever written, whose melody is known by all and whose words are understood by few.

Ambrose of Milan (n.): *Church Father* (q.v.) who converted St. Augustine, invented the *Hymn* (q.v.), and was the first person in history recorded to have been able to read without moving his lips (as opposed to without moving his gray matter, the method adopted by most contemporary Christians).

Amen (expletive): A multipurpose ejaculation that can mean things like, "You can say that again!", "Ain't that right?", and "O.K., you can wake up now; the *Prayer* (q.v.) and/or *Service* (q.v.) is over."

When the Preacher's particular spin
Zeroes in on the horrible sin
    That's afflicting Another,
    We shout, "Preach it, brother!
Hear, Hear! Preach it, brother! *Amen.*"

Amnesia (n.): A medical condition which afflicts the *Congregation* (q.v.) within minutes after the ending of the *Sermon* (q.v.); which may explain why they return the next week to hear yet another one.

Amplification (n.): A method used by *Worship Teams* (q.v.) in churches singing contemporary *Praise and Worship* music (q.v.) to render the *Congregation* (q.v.) superfluous. It solves the problem of whether or not the people are participating in the singing by making it impossible to tell.

Angel (n.): Spiritual beings with wings and haloes whose function is to deliver messages from God, dance on the heads of pins, and appear disguised as human beings on TV shows. They are apparently born as chubby little boys but grow up to be slim, beautiful women with long hair. When off duty, they like to lie around on clouds and play harps.

Angel, Guardian (n.): an *Angel* (q.v.) in charge of preventing some particular human being from destroying himself. They tend to rest up from such arduous assignments by doing something relatively easy, like pushing planets around the sun, cleaning out black holes, or keeping track of all the electrons in a galaxy.

Announcements (n.): That point in the *Service* (q.v.) when the information is given orally that was ignored when presented in written form (see *Bulletin*).

Anselm of Canterbury (n.): *Church Father* (q.v.) who proved conclusively that, if there is a God, then He exists. Cf. *Ontological Argument*.

Answers from Aslan: The Enduring Apologetics of C. S. Lewis. Tampa: DeWard, 2024 (n.): Attempt by that insufferable scholar *Donald T. Williams* (q.v.) to update Lewis's apologetic arguments for the Twenty-First Century. Almost as bad as the material it purports to study.

Anthem (n.): A musical performance inflicted by the *Choir* (q.v.) on the *Congregation* (q.v.) in retaliation for the *Congregation's* refusal to join the *Choir* on the *Hymns* (q.v.).

Anti-Christ (n.): The current offering of the Villain of the Month Club. Past selections (who can always be resurrected for another run) include The Pope, Hitler, Mussolini, Stalin, Richard Nixon, Henry Kissinger, Saddam Hussein, Billy Graham, Bill Clinton, Bill Gates, Barack Obama, and Donald Trump. Donald T. Williams, PhD, is *obviously* ineligible for selection because he steadfastly maintains that he did not write this Dictionary.

Anti-Intellectualism (n.) The woman who is married to Uncle Intellectualism. Their long and rocky marriage led the poet George Gordon, Lord Byron, to infamously rhyme "intellectual" with "hen pecked, you all." Somehow, Anti has managed to become a member of every *Fundamentalist* (q.v.) and *Evangelical* (q.v.) church in America, where, in spite of the level of mental energy required to evade Jesus' version of the Great Commandment, she shows she is up to the task.

> The Thought Police will inspect you all,
> Interrogate and dissect you all
> Lest the horrible plague should infect you all
> Which has threatened e'er now to have wrecked you all.
> If it has, they will surely detect you all
> And pursue you until they have decked you all.
> Your excuses will prove ineffectual
> And the members will rightly reject you all
> For trying to be intellectual.

Though I really can't say I have checked you all,
With all of these rhymes, I expect you all
To be duly impressed
By my passing the test
And not using Lord Byron's "hen pecked, you all."

Apologetics 1 (n., archaic): The rational defense of the faith, supporting evangelism aimed at the whole person, including the mind; 2 (n., current): The ministry of arguing about how to defend the faith in support of evangelism, thereby avoiding both defense and evangelism while seeming to engage in them both.

Apostle 1 (n., archaic): An eyewitness to the Resurrection appointed by Christ as a foundational teacher of Christian doctrine; 2 (n., current): any denominational official whose ego exceeds twice the legal limit.

Application (n.): That part of the *Sermon* (q.v.) in which the practical relevance of the Text for life is explained. The application of all passages of Scripture can basically be reduced to four points: Get Saved, Be Baptized, Join the Church, and Rededicate your Life. Anything else would be a dilution of the *Altar Call* (q.v.) and therefore inappropriate.

After one has come down for Salvation,
Baptism, and Rededication,
What's then left to do
But stare at your shoe
While growth suffers sad suffocation?

Approach the Throne of Grace (v., t.): To *Pray* (q.v.), especially when an extra measure of pomposity is desired.

Aquinas, Thomas (n.): Medieval *Theologian* (q.v.) who divided the subject matter of *Theology* (q.v.) into 42,859 Questions, each having approximately 2,137 possible Answers, with an average of 1,242 Reasons For and 1,242 Reasons Against each Answer, each explained in exhaustive detail using an average of 34,876 Latin words consisting of an average of 4.13 syllables each. Scholars have been using high-speed computer searches for the last two decades in an attempt to find whether Aquinas imbedded a Final Answer somewhere in the text. All this he modestly referred to as a Summary.

Archangel (n.): A higher level of *Angel* (q.v.), so called because of their tendency to hang around the arches of *Gothic* (q.v.) churches.

Aristotle (n.): Ancient *Philosopher* (q.v.), disciple of *Plato* (q.v.), who translated the *Summa Theologica* of *Thomas Aquinas* (q.v.) into Greek.

Arminius, Jacobus (n.): No-point Calvinist who was predestined to oppose the doctrine of Election. Cf. *Calvin, John*.

Arminian (n.): One who has never read *Arminius* (q.v.) or *Calvin* (q.v.), but who objects to the caricature of *Calvinism* (q.v.) projected by those followers of *Calvin* who have never read *Arminius* either, but who nonetheless endeavor to defend their master in his charges against Calvinism by making *Calvin* appear to have been right. Cf. *Point*.

Arminianism (n.): The doctrine that *Calvin* (q.v.) was wrong, even where *Arminius* (q.v.) would have agreed with him.

Arts, the (n.): Exercises in hoity-toity pride and obnoxious superiority, such as the creation, performance, or enjoyment of classical music, painting, sculpture, poetry, drama, cinema, etc. At best, they are frivolous wastes of time; more often, enticements to evil; always, manifestations of spiritual pride.

Arts, Contemporary (n.): A cabal of those practitioners of the *Arts* (q. v.) now living, many of whom are dedicated to providing some excuse for the typical Christian attitude toward the *Arts* in general.

> We are Artists! Thus, we cannot be
> Bound to any false conformity
> To Nature (or to Grammar, for that matter);
> It is enough if we keep up the chatter.
> For we are *Artists*! Therefore what we say
> Has worth intrinsic. Things are just that way.
> And if our works cannot be understood,
> Well, we think that is all more to the good
> Because by this they seem the more profound,
> Whereby our reputations do abound.
> Don't worry whether what we say is true;
> It's more important that it just be new!
> Each emotion in our hearts that flowers
> Makes worthwhile reading just because it's ours.
> Edification, timeless truth, insight,
> Whether our sentiments are wrong or right,
> We can't be bothered by such bourgeois fetters,
> For we are Great Men—Artists—Men of Letters!
> Dump the raw emotions on the sheet
> To make a lyric poem that can't be beat.
> Look, look: we have no tune, and yet we sing!
> Oh, come and hear. It is the latest thing.

Asceticism (n.): That form of *Abstinence* (q.v.) practiced by monks, nuns, and hermits; not as spiritual as the Fundamentalist versions, which are capable of inconveniencing not only the abstainers themselves but also everyone around them.

Associate Pastor (n.): A functionary in the Church who does most of the work and gets half of the pay and none of the credit.

Assonance (n.): The repetition of vowel sounds, i.e., the braying of asses in the *Sermon* (q.v.).

> There once was a prominent Preacher
> Whose most recognizable feature
>   Was taut vocal chords
>   Sharp as two edged swords:
> A right homiletical Screacher!

Atheism (n.): The doctrine that there is no God, or, that if there is, He will certainly be too ashamed ever to show His face in the world, given the nature of His followers, so we might as well live as if there is none.

Atheist (n.): A person who is so disgusted—or has been so wounded—by the inconsistent lifestyles, gracelessness, and intellectual foolishness of most Christians that he cannot hear the witness of the others.

Attendance (n.): Showing up; one of the surest ways to attain *Merit* (q.v.) and *Salvation* (q.v.).

Augustine of Canterbury (n.): *Church Father* (q.v.) who was sent by Pope Gregory the Great to evangelize the Angles and Saxons after Gregory had mistaken them for angels in the Roman slave market. This attempt to salvage papal infallibility gave us the Church of England.

Augustine of Hippo (n.): *Church Father* (q.v.) who refuted *Pelagius* (q.v.) by crying as a baby, stealing pears, and having a mistress. Though certain theological arguments were also involved, the practical refutation remains convincing anyway. He also invented the autobiography and the confessional.

Auto da Fe (n.): "Act of faith"; a form of *Church Discipline* (q.v.) which Roman Catholics historically used to get all fired up about (see *Spanish Inquisition; Burning at the Stake; Flame War*); the Catholic method of turning problem members into Hot Gospelers. After cooling down from this heart-warming experience, the former heretics become the Dead Orthodox.

> The Grand Inquisitor
> Was seldom a welcome visitor.
> His penchant for barbecued sinner
> Could be rather awkward at dinner.

Avant Garde (adj.): Belonging to that group of Artists who wish to make offending their elders (and contemporaries, for that matter) the primary purpose of their work, rather than merely a pleasant side-effect. Unfortunately, this can be a rather self-defeating proposition.

> When trying to sell his new fictions,
> He cast off all social restrictions.
> But his efforts were blocked
> When no one was shocked;
> They no longer had any convictions.

Axiology (n.): In *Philosophy* (q.v.), the study of fundamental values; so named after the axes ground by the participants.

B

Babel, Tower of (n.): Ancient site of the founding of the Pentecostal Movement; thought to have been erected in Azusa Street.

Babylon Bee, The (n.): The only non-fake news source left in the post-truth age. It presents only simple, unadulterated facts without the least hint of commentary, hyperbole, or (especially) sarcasm.

Balm in Gilead (n.): An ancient spelling for an explosive device planted by the Palestine Liberation Organization.

Baptism (n.): A ritual ablution whose original purpose was to mark off Christians from the rest of the world, but which has since been adapted to the much more important use of distinguishing them from one another. See *Effusion, Immersion, Spargation*.

Baptist (n.): One who believes in the Five Fundamentals of the Faith: the Dunking of Converts; the Eternal Security of the Believer; the Extension of Altar Calls; the Tithing of Money; and the Splitting of Churches.

Baptist, Independent 1 (n.): A redundancy, like ugly American, greedy Capitalist, or born Sucker. See *Redundant*. 2 (n.): A member of a *Denomination* (q.v.) of Christians who are proud of not belonging to any *Denomination*.

Baptistry (n.): A tank, usually mounted in a recessed alcove in the wall behind the *Choir Loft* (q.v.), in which new converts are dunked (see *Baptism*). Frequently the back wall of the alcove will be covered by a mural of the River Jordan flowing through the English countryside.

Barf, Karl: Swiss theologian and guru of Neo-Orthodoxy, so named for the gustatory reaction which follows from the attempt to digest the turgid prose in his massive, 148-volume systematic theology, which was as full of logical holes as his national cheese (created, in both cases, by the expansion of various gases). Sometimes unaccountably spelled *Barth*.

That great theologian, Karl Barth,
Wrote with deep philosophical art:
He thought that the Word
Was both God's and absurd,
For his mind was half Paul and half Sartre.

Behaviorism (n.): An alternative explanation to *Free Will* (q.v.) for the follies of mankind; the theory that the universe is a giant Skinner Box and all the men and women merely rodents.

A psychologist named B. F. Skinner
Said that Man was *conditioned* a sinner.
He proved it with stats
He collected from rats
Who were there just to get the free dinner.

Benedict of Nursia (n.): The inventor of *Monasticism* (q.v.) and the church *Nursery* (q.v.); also thought by many scholars to have been the ghost-writer of *Robert's Rules of Order*.

Benedict Option 1 (n.): A strategy whereby the church is supposed to hide from the world in the hope that it will not be noticed; thought first to have been proposed by Benedict Arnold. 2 (n.): The title of a book which does not *exactly* recommend the strategy in definition 1.

Benediction (n.): The signal for a mad dash to prevent the pot roast from becoming a *Burnt Offering* (q.v.).

> Whatever the subtle restriction
> That inhibits mass auto-eviction,
>   It's taken away
>   When we hear someone say,
> "Please rise for the Benediction."

Benevolence Offering (n.): The buying up by the rich of salve for the conscience at bargain basement prices.

Bible (n.): An ancient book, the primary source of *Prooftexts* (q.v.). Belief-statements by Christians are ostensibly supposed to be based on this book. For various strategies for making this appear to be so, see numerous definitions in this Dictionary.

Bible App (n.): A program that allows one to access *Prooftexts* (q.v.) from one's phone. This is considered a great advance over the Bible itself, as it facilitates correcting *Heretics* (q.v.) on *Facebook* (q.v.).

Bible Study (n.): An oxymoron (as the two words are used by most contemporary Christians). See *Study Bible*.

Bickerstaff, Isaac (n.): Eighteenth-century author who ghost-wrote much material for Addison and Steele, and whose observations on London society had no influence whatsoever on *The Devil's Dictionary of the Christian Church*.

Bierce, Ambrose (n.): Early twentieth-century journalist, novelist, raconteur, church historian, and curmudgeon whose masterpiece, *The Devil's Dictionary*, neither inspired nor had any influence whatsoever on *The Devil's Dictionary of the Christian Church*.

Bildad the Shoe Height (n.): The shortest man in the *Bible* (q.v.).

Bishop (n.): An ecclesiastical instance of the Pointy-Haired Boss syndrome. See *Miter, Dilbert.*

Bird, The 1 (n.): An obscene gesture which is *never* used by Christians unless someone pulls out in front of them in traffic, which is entirely different; 2 (n.): The "Bird and Baby," local nickname for the "Eagle and Child," the pub in Oxford where the *Inklings* (q.v.) met to plot the overthrow of true Christianity by writing books with witches and wizards in them.

Board (n.): A group of old men whose function is to ensure that the Church will continue to use only those methods of ministry which were successful with the generation now deceased.

Board Meeting (n.): A misspelling of Bored Meeting; A gathering of the *Board* (q.v.) for the purposes of *Gossip* (q.v.), grandstanding, and obstruction.

Book of Common Prayer (n.): A document sections of which are unthinkingly mumbled by Anglicans/Episcopalians every week; the source from which other Protestants steal when they wish to feign dignity.

Bookstore (n.): A store that sells books. The best ones are Rare.

"Do not open!" reads the warning
On the annotated glass.
Leather covers, gold adorning
Kept by polished wood and brass.
"Do not touch; request assistance."
Just admiring from a distance
Fortifies my sales resistance.
Virgil, with a mild insistence
Whispers, "Look and pass."

Bookstore, Christian (n.): A commercial establishment which sells tapes, compact discs, tacky knick-knacks, sentimental, clumsily edifying posters, cutesy bumper stickers, statuettes of infantile-looking angels, incredibly expensive greeting cards, and cheap jewelry. It is thought that the name reflects the ancient practice of reading books, believed once to have been sold in these establishments; but this practice has long since been given up by contemporary Christians.

Bull, Papal (n.): An official proclamation by the *Pope* (q.v.) which adds to the Deposit of Faith; so named from its resemblance to deposits left by certain large bovine mammals.

Bulletin (n.): A document which attempts to present in written form that information which is ignored when presented orally (see *Announcements*).

Burning at the Stake (n.): A method of shedding light on theological disputes which could produce rather sizzling results. See *Auto da Fe, Flame War*.

Burnt Offering (n.): What the pot roast becomes as a result of the *Altar Call* (q.v.).

Business, Necessary (n): a service without which Society cannot function or exist during a *Pandemic* (q.v.). Necessary businesses include massage parlors, bars, and tattoo shops, but not police departments, schools, or churches.

Byzantine (adj.): Pertaining to the Eastern Empire which, acknowledging neither the fall of (political) Rome nor the rise of (ecclesiastical) Rome, continued to do its own thing for a thousand years while giving birth to Eastern *Orthodoxy* (q.v.).

Byzantium (n.): That city which is Istanbul, not Constantinople; but that's nobody's business but the Turks.

C

Call 1 (n.): The illusion, produced by the combination of guilt overload and sensory deprivation at *Altar Calls* (q. v.), that one ought to deny everything one knows about one's actual gifts, inclinations, or abilities, and become a *Preacher* (q. v.) or *Missionary* (q. v.) anyway. 2 (v., t.): To hire the *Candidate* (q. v.) on the specious assumption that he will be able to continue performing up to the Congregation's expectations.

Calvin, John (n.): Protestant Reformer who chose to deny free will. Cf. *Arminius, Jacobus*.

Calvinism (n.): The doctrine that *Arminius* (q.v.) was wrong, even where *Calvin* (q.v.) would have agreed with him.

Calvinist (n.): One who thinks he is following *John Calvin* (q.v.) by accepting the decision of *Arminius* (q.v.) to take five points of *Calvin's* theology out of context for purposes of attempted refutation.

Canon (n.): The official list of those books recognized as part of *Scripture* (q.v.); so named because they are the source of the ammunition (cf. *Prooftext*) for the artillery used in theological warfare.

Candidate 1 (v., i.): To audition for the position of *Preacher* (q. v.) by giving a sermon which one has actually worked on (cf. *Preparation*). Once the Preacher has been hired, the Church will of course see to it that such *Preparation* will become impossible to schedule, which will lead to the next occasion of *Candidating*. 2 (n.): The person doing the *Candidating*.

Cardinal (n.): High Roman Catholic officials and advisers to the *Pope* (q.v.) with red hats. Why the St. Louis professional baseball team is given this kind of ecclesiastical influence has never been adequately explained.

Carpet (n.): A floor covering, the color of which has been the cause of innumerable *Church Splits* (q.v.).

> With faces as smug as the mug of a thug,
> With sounds like the snarling of pit-bull or pug,
> We pursue the to-do
> O'er the shade of the hue
> That the Board recommends for replacing the rug.

Catholic 1 (n.): A member of the one, true, holy, and apostolic Church. They know this because the Church has told them so, which must be true, for said Church also claims to be infallible. 2 (adj.): Pertaining to Catholicism; addicted to smells and bells and having a blind faith in the veracity and consistency of the official pronouncements of the long line of saints, heretics, rogues, fools, and knaves who have occupied the papal throne.

Cemetery (n.): A plot of land, often adjacent to or behind the *Sanctuary* (q.v.), where the bodies of *Members* (q.v.) are deposited when they have become as lifeless as their spirits were while in the *Sanctuary*.

Cemetery, Theological (n.): A more accurate spelling of *Seminary* (q.v.).

Chapel 1 (n.): A compulsory Study Hall masquerading as a Worship Service in the school day of the *Christian College* (q.v.). Those students who do not face imminent exams may read their mail instead. 2 (n.):

A small *Sanctuary* (q.v.) jutting off from the main *Sanctuary* in a liturgical church, just to keep things confu—er, interesting.

Charity 1 (n., archaic): Sacrificial and unconditional love, modeled on that of God. 2 (n., current): Giving to the poor (cf. *Benevolence Offering*), especially if done in a public, condescending, and patronizing manner.

Chastity 1 (n., archaic): Sexual continence outside of marriage and faithfulness within it. 2 (n., current): Unknown.

Chesterton G. K. (n.): British writer who invented the *Oxymoron* (q.v.) and the *Paradox* (q.v.). Since he was possessed of wit and humor, he is obviously a bad influence.

Chiasmus (n.): A rhetorical device, used in the Psalms, in which the author says something and then says it again backwards; seldom used by contemporary Christians, because they do most things backwards in the first place.

Child-rearing (n.): The period of sleeplessness, self-flagellation, servitude, guilt, and seminar attending that follows breeding.

Children's Church (n.): A place for the incarceration of pre-adolescents during the *Service* (q.v.) so that they will not see the Emperor's New Clothes.

Choir, Church (n.): A device for mangling musical compositions; an organization whose purpose is to be late for practice and to ensure that the Church is never accused of the horrible crime of committing one of the *Arts* (q.v.). At least one member is required to be both very loud and very tone deaf. This provides the opportunity for the other members to discuss these failings behind the person's back, but never kindly to suggest another ministry for said person lest he or she be offended, and, besides, he or she is making a "joyful noise" and thereby being more *spiritual* (q.v.) than those who can actually sing.

Choir, College (n.): An attempt to render aspiring vocalists unfit for service in Church Choirs.

Choir Director (n.): A member, often of such a gross and degraded temperament as to be in danger of committing one of the *Arts* (q.v.), who is punished for this regrettable tendency by being given this job in order to mortify his flesh and keep him humble. In particularly recalcitrant cases, he may also be asked to serve as *Song Leader* (q.v.).

Choir Loft 1 (n.): A game, similar to tossing the caber, but using choir members or the director; often played at *Church Picnics* (q.v.) after a particularly execrable performance. 2 (n.): In church architecture, the elevated heights from which the *Choir* descends to infiltrate the congregation during the singing of the final *Hymn* (q.v.) before the *Sermon* (q.v.).

Choir Practice (n.): An exercise in futility; the attempt to teach a different group of people from the ones who will show up on Sunday how to sing the anthems, etc., planned for that Sunday's *Service* (q.v.).

Choir Robe (n.): A futile attempt to restore visually to the *Choir* (q.v.) members some of the semblance of dignity lost aurally in their performance.

Chorus 1 (n.): A repetitive section which separates the verses of *Hymns* (q.v.) in an attempt to compensate for the verses left out.

2 (n.): In *Contemporary Christian Music* (q.v.), a hymn, as it were, which has no verses. 3 (n.): In *The Messiah* (q.v.), the less boring parts.

Christian 1 (n., archaic): One who believes that Jesus Christ is Lord and is prepared to live and die for that belief; 2 (n., current, Conservative): One who believes that Jesus Christ is Lord and is prepared to condemn others for not believing it exactly as he does; 3 (n., current, Liberal): One who does not believe anything in particular about Jesus but has gotten used to the label and sees no reason to discard it; 4 (adj., archaic): Attached to, associated with, or bearing a likeness to Jesus Christ; characterized by the endeavor, however imperfect, to live as his disciple; 5 (adj., current): Approved (or disapproved, as the case may be) by the speaker.

Christian Love (n.): An *Oxymoron* (q.v.); the state of caring enough about someone to include him or her in the list of those about whom or to whom you *gossip* (q.v.).

Christian Music Industry (n.): A commercial enterprise whose purpose is to produce cheap imitations of secular musical styles with innocuous lyrics; money; and divorces.

Christian Nationalist (n.): A Christian whose politics is one inch to the right or one's own.

Christian Perfection (n.): The doctrine, promulgated by *John Wesley* (q.v.), that if you are not aware of any sin in your life, there isn't any there. Cf. *Sanctification, Entire.*

Christian Romance Novel (n.): Poorly written fiction in which the main characters consist of one handsome, troubled agnostic male and one beautiful, co-dependent religious female. The plot revolves around the male overcoming his problems, being converted, and marrying the female in a matter of days (or hours), whereupon they live happily ever after. The purpose of these novels is apparently to entice religious women into "missionary dating," thus ensuring that they will marry an immature and unstable male. They will then need an escape from their life with him, which they will find in continuing to read said novels.

Christian Subculture (n.): The species of kitsch sold in Christian Bookstores (cf. *Bookstore, Christian*). Denominations differ on the style of tackiness preferred. The Eastern Orthodox gravitate to flat cartoon portraits of Jesus scowling from the Right Hand of the Father; Roman Catholics favor effeminate martyrs who apparently enjoy being stuck with arrows or boiled in oil; Fundamentalists prefer preachy placards prominently packed with puerile platitudes; and Evangelical Protestants like infantile angels who could not say, "Fear not!" with credibility to a wooly worm.

Christian Worldview (n.): The way in which thinking Christians, aligning their thinking with Scripture, would, if there were any, allegedly look at the world. In the *Christian Liberal Arts College* (q.v.), this is usually achieved by opening class with *Prayer* (q.v.) and sprinkling Evangelical *Jargon* (q.v.) liberally throughout the lecture; in the *Bible College* (q.v.), one does not look at the world.

Christianity Today (n.): A popular Christian magazine which was founded for the purpose of encouraging pastors to engage with serious Christian thought, and which has been fleeing that purpose like the plague ever since. In the first volume, the major articles were written by the greatest living American Evangelical theologian; the greatest living European Evangelical theologian; and the greatest living British Bible scholar. In the latest issue, they were written by a journalist; a journalist; and a journalist.

Christmas (n.): A pagan holiday which, because it uses the standard English spelling of *Christ*, is able to mask the fact that it really *is* part of a vast conspiracy to take Christ out of Christmas. Cf. *Xmas*.

Church Bus (n.): A means of transportation which doubles as a proof that miracles have not ceased, whenever the Youth Group returns from an outing.

Church Business Meeting (n.): The public phase of *Church Government* (q.v.), designed to produce the illusion that the real thing has not in fact already been conducted behind closed doors. A typical agenda includes: *Prayer* (q.v.); acknowledging and voting on any new members; failing to mention or delete from the rolls any old members who have died, moved away, or just disappeared into the woodwork, never to be seen or heard from again; hurrying past the financial report; reporting exaggerated and unrealistic statistics on how many doors the Visitation Team has knocked on and how many Conversions they have recorded; neglecting to explain where all these alleged converts are; Old Business and New Business (which primarily consist of rubber-stamping any grandiose schemes which the Unofficial Ruling Clique favors and shooting down any intelligent ideas they oppose); adjournment.

Church Camp (n.): A vacation for Christian adults from the rigors of *Child-rearing* (q.v.).

Church Discipline 1 (n., archaic): The act of lovingly confronting those who sin, with restoration as the goal, then involving the elders if repentance does not follow, finally moving to excommunication as a tragic last resort; 2 (n., Roman Catholic): The *Spanish Inquisition*; *Autos da Fe* (q.v.); 3 (n., Cultic): Shunning; 4 (n., Protestant Fundamentalist): Character assassination; 5 (n., Protestant Liberal/

Mainline): "If we adopt the heresy or immorality in question, it won't be heretical or immoral any more." 6 (n., Protestant Evangelical): "If we ignore the problem long enough, it will go away."

Church Fathers 1 (n.): The members of Promise Keepers; 2 (n.): Leaders of the Church who lived between the Apostles and the Fall of Rome. After that, they were entering into their Middle Ages and becoming grandfathers.

Church Government (n.): The art of convincing the *Congregation* (q.v.) that they have freely chosen what the ruling clique on the Board of Deacons (or Board of Elders, or Bishop, or District Superintendent, depending on the denominational structure) has already decided in advance.

Church Growth (n.): The ability of a given congregation to fulfill its mission by expanding its statistics. What causes one church to grow as opposed to another remains something of a mystery, but a number of theories have been offered, for example: A. There are three factors: the Parking Lot, the Nursery, and the Women's Bathroom; B. There are three factors: Location, Location, and Location; C. Make sure that all the members are just like all the other members; D. It's the Programs, stupid. These views may not be mutually exclusive. The one thing that seems certain is that, once significant Growth has begun, the Lemming Effect will probably cause it to continue until the next *Church Split* (q. v.).

Church League (n.): The Protestant version of the *Indulgence* (q.v.); in return for the Entry Fee, one is granted a partial and temporary dispensation of the prohibition of profanity, in case of an unfavorable call by an Official.

Church Picnic (n.): A device for illustrating the evils of combining gluttony with softball. See *Heave Offering*; *Potluck*.

Church Split (n.): A form of asexual ecclesiastical reproduction; cf. *Mitosis*.

Church Year (n.): The cycle of traditional religious festivals and observances which includes Christmas, The New Year's Eve Watchnight Service, Super-Bowl Sunday, Easter, Mother's Day, Father's Day, Independence Day, Labor Day, and Turkey Day.

Clergy (n.): The management of an ecclesiastical establishment; distinguished from the *Laity* (q.v.) either by collars, ties, or bad hair, depending on the *Denomination* (q.v.).

Clerical (adj.): Pertaining to the *Clergy* (q.v.), as in collars, vestments, or scandals.

Clerihew (n.): A form of *Poetry* (q.v.) in which the first line is the name of a famous person and the others, rhyming AABB, make a snide comment about him or her; named after its inventor, Edmund Clerihew Bentley, a friend of G. K. Chesterton. Such a crude verse form would obviously only be used by deviants or social degenerates such as humorists and satirists, and hence has no place at all in this Dictionary.

Edmund C. Bentley
Was called, evidently
By Clio the Muse
To invent clerihews.
(He did not refuse.)

Cloning (n.): A method of reproduction which the Church considers inappropriate for humans, though it is quite willing to use it for converts, congregations, programs, or ministers.

Collection (n.): Another word for the *Offering* (q.v.), apparently from the fact that in non-liturgical churches this most important part of the service replaces the Collects.

Collection Plate (n.): A brass dish lined with velvet, used as a receptacle for small bills and change.

College (n.): See *University*.

College, Bible (n.): *Sunday School* (q.v.) conducted during the week; distinguished from *Daily Vacation Bible School* (q.v.) by the age of the students and by the fact that it lasts longer than one week and does not meet in the summer; distinguished from *Church Camp* (q.v.) by the same features.

College, Christian (n.): An *Oxymoron* (q.v.); a place to which young people are sent to be protected from any contact with the *World* (q.v.) so that they may thereby learn effectively to minister to it. These institutions take two main forms: the *Bible College* (q.v.) and the *Christian Liberal Arts College* (q.v.).

College, Christian Liberal Arts (n.): An institution that used to be a *Bible College* (q.v.) but has not yet become a secular university.

College President (n.): A functionary who is given the primary responsibility for keeping a *Christian College* (q.v.) spiritually focused and faithful to its mission because of his ability to raise money.

Comfortable (adj.): Enjoying a state of intellectual and emotional sloth untroubled by unpleasant external considerations; the ultimate criterion for ethical decisions, as in the sentence, "I'm not comfortable with that."

Commentary (n.): A book whose purpose is to have light shed on it by the Bible.

Communion 1 (n.): The state of being in fellowship close enough to facilitate *Gossip* (q.v.); 2 (n.): What non-theologians call the *Eucharist* (q.v.) or *Lord's Supper* (q.v.); from the communion with their navels which usually takes place concurrently.

Complementarianism (n.): The teaching that men and women are just the same, only different. Cf. *Egalitarianism* and *Hierarchicalism*.

Conclusion (n.): That part of the *Sermon* (q.v.) which must be announced at least three times before it actually begins.

It certainly is an illusion
That reliably leads to confusion
When, three or four times,
Like clockwork that chimes,
The Preacher intones, "In conclusion ..."

Concordance (n.): The apparatus which allows one to find the *Prooftexts* (q.v.) in Scripture without actually having to read it.

Concert (n.): The attempt by the *Christian Music Industry* (q.v.) to render its patrons too deaf to realize how badly it is cheating them out of both music and Christianity.

Conditional Immortality (n.): The doctrine that *Hell* (q.v.) only seems to last forever.

Confession (n.): The act of owning up to one's *Sins* (q.v.) in order to ask for forgiveness and seek absolution; addressed by archaic Christians to God, by Roman Catholics to a *Priest* (q.v.), and by modern Christians to a talk-show host.

> When trying to make our confession
> We should surely avoid the impression
> (Which would be somewhat rude)
> Of a mere interlude
> Before getting on with regression.

Confession of Faith (n.): A document setting forth the official doctrinal commitments of a given *Denomination* (q.v.) so that *Fundamentalists* (q.v.) will know what to misunderstand, *Evangelicals* (q.v.) what to rationalize, and *Liberals* (q.v.) what to ignore.

Congregation (n.): Church-speak for *Audience*; those who show up for the entertainment offered on any given Sunday.

Conroy, Melissa (n.): Former student and secretary of *Donald T. Williams* (q.v.), who has no sense of humor whatsoever and did not contribute any definitions (such as *Christian Romance Novel* or *Crying*) to this Dictionary.

Conscience (n.): The warning system in the brain which reminds us of the dangers of failing to conform to the expectations of the group we are trying to impress.

Contemporary Christian Music (n.): A form of caterwauling in which simple, repetitive words expressing vague, repetitive ideas are set to simple, repetitive tunes and reiterated ad infinitum. The effect is similar to that of the *mantras* of Eastern religions: to induce a state of ecstatic stupefaction euphemistically known as "praise and worship."

Context (n.): That which is ignored in interpretation.

Contrition (n.): The public display that follows Getting Caught.

Conversion (n.): The act of yielding to social and emotional pressure and replacing one system of nonsense, foolishness, and chicanery with another.

Convert 1 (n.): A *Sheep* (q.v.) which has been stolen recently; 2 (v., t.): To find an unsuspecting victim and make him twice the son of perdition as oneself.

Counseling (n.): The ministry of providing fools and incompetents with various terms of psychological jargon which they can then use to excuse or justify their irresponsibility and misbehavior.

Counter-Reformation 1 (n.): Replacing the formica tops in the Church Kitchen; 2 (n.): The attempt by the Roman Catholic Church to close the Barn Door after the horses had already been driven to another pasture; the moment in the Sixteenth Century when the Catholic Church attempted to purify itself by kicking out everyone who subscribed to the following heretical tenets: (A) God offers forgiveness in response to repentance and faith rather than the payment of money; (B) The Bible means what the Prophets and Apostles intended it to mean when they wrote it; (C) God meant the *Members* (q.v.) to understand what was going on in the *Service* (q.v.).

Credo: Meditations on the Nicene Creed. Middletown, RI: Stone Tower Press, 2025 (n.): A book in which archaic wannabe *Donald T. Williams* (q.v.), who had nothing whatsoever to do with the composition of this Dictionary, tries to elucidate and apply the meaning of The Nicene Creed for the church today. Reading this book should be avoided at all costs, for it can only have the effect of deepening your spiritual life and putting you completely out of step with contemporary Christendom.

Creed (n.): That which is recited in the service and ignored in the bureaucracy.

> The saints who once would burn and bleed
> Rather than deny the Creed
> Now pay no heed to what they say,
> Though still they say it anyway.

Critic (n.): One who practices *Biblical Criticism* (q.v.); or, anyone who talks about the *Preacher* (q.v.), especially behind his back.

Critical Race Theory (n.): The doctrine that it is a sin to attend events sponsored by NASCAR. The races are socially constructed to be won disproportionately by white good ol' boys, and denials or counter-evidence only prove that the theory is true because white racers are blinded by their own whiteness. The observation that the theory appears to be as circular as the races is strictly forbidden as racist in itself.

Criticism (n.): Language which points out the faults of its subject. *Constructive Criticism* is that which one makes of others; *Harsh* or *Unjustified Criticism* is that which others make of us.

Criticism, Biblical (n.): The science of proving that various bits of the Bible were not written until after people had been reading them for several hundred years; a conspiracy to deny intellectual respectability to anyone who does not subscribe to the following premises: (A) No ancient writer could ever possibly have known any synonyms for anything; (B) No ancient itinerant preacher could ever possibly have reused any of his material, and if he did, he was required to repeat it verbatim; (C) No omnipotent Being is capable of acting, no omniscient Being is capable of imparting knowledge, and no Being who created the tongue is capable of speaking in articulate language.

> A high-critical biblical scholar
> Wrote books that all caused quite a holler:
> He claimed that St. Paul
> Wrote *The Campaigns of Gaul,*
> And he made about three million dollars.

Cruciform (adj.): Shaped like a cross; in church architecture, considered an appropriate form as corresponding with the fact that their association with the visible church is so often such a heavy cross for the godly to bear.

Crying (n.): A specific tongue (cf. *Glossolalia*) spoken primarily by women, most often during public *Testimonies* (q.v.), the preamble to the *Special Music* (q.v.), or praying. Unlike other unknown tongues, crying is accepted in all denominations and is not required to be interpreted.

Culture (n.): That part of *The World* (q.v.) which is the abode of *The Arts* (q.v.); therefore unredeemable and to be especially avoided.

Culture War (n.): The attempt by Christian conservatives to reverse the effects of their failure to pursue evangelism and discipleship without reversing their failure as evangelists and disciple makers.

Cultured Despisers of Religion (n.): The effect produced when Newton's Law meets the Religious Despisers of Culture.

D

Daily Vacation Bible School (n.): Where school children bored by summer vacation put up with extra *Sunday School* (q.v.) in order to get the Kool-Aid and Oreos.

Damnation (n.): Being sent to Hell everlastingly for one's sins. All human beings deserve damnation, but some deserve it more than others, the speaker least of all.

Dante (n.): Medieval tourist who was exiled when his Florentine neighbors got tired of his incessant pestering them to come over to his house and see the slides of his trip through *Hell* (q.v.), *Purgatory* (q.v.), and *Heaven* (q.v.). Frustrated in these efforts, he turned to writing and produced a travelogue which became a best seller. Many of those offending former neighbors are depicted being roasted, fried, barbecued, broiled, fricasseed, or shish-kabobbed by various demons devoted to the culinary arts. Later, this became the inspiration for diverse cooking shows on TV, such as "The Iron Chef."

Daylight Savings Time (n.): That which occupies almost twice as much of the year as so-called "standard" time; that which causes people to be even more late for church than usual on one Sunday in the Spring; that which is the only thing that can cause them to be early, but only on one Sunday in the Fall.

Twice a year we have to find the knack
Of springing forward or of falling back.

The time is out of joint; we cannot keep
The daily rhythm of our nightly sleep.
We need the extra hour (Do the math!)
To keep the Sun from setting on our wrath
At being jerked awake while in the dark.
Since Noah let the critters off the ark,
The Seasons managed, without help from us,
To change throughout the year without a fuss.
But now, without an act of Congress, they
(Forget the year!) can't tell the time of day.

Deacon (n.): An ecclesiastical functionary who, in the Episcopal Church, is not quite a *Priest* (q.v.) and therefore has no power at all, but who, in the Baptist Church, is not quite an *Elder* (q.v.) and can therefore run the Elder out of town.

Dead Orthodoxy (n.): A redundancy, like tooth dentist, foolish person, or bad pun. See *redundant*.

Decently and in Order 1 (adv.): An obscure approach to *Church Government* (q.v.), last attempted at the Jerusalem Council. 2 (adv.): An obscure approach to worship, last attempted in the Upper Room; not to be confused with boring the congregation to death or whipping it into a frenzy, the highly superior approaches which have thankfully replaced it.

Deconstruction 1 (n.): The theory that all language (except that of the Deconstructionist) contains the inherent negation of its own truth claims, and that therefore no language (except that of the Deconstructionist when he is explaining this) is capable of communicating anything about any world outside the language system itself. Therefore, all academic prose should be as incomprehensible as possible in order to hide the fact that it is not talking about anything except itself. If the Deconstructionist finds any language that is not incomprehensible, it is his duty to render it so by "deconstructing" it. See *Derrida, Post-Modernism,* etc. 2 (n.): The act of reconsidering one's beliefs in order to bring them into conformity with the Spirit of the Age.

Deeper Magic: The Theology behind the Writings of C S. Lewis. Baltimore: Square Halo Books, 2016. (n.): Disastrous effort by that insufferable archaic wannabe *Donald T. Williams* (q.v.) to assess the strengths and weaknesses of *Lewis* (q.v.) as a teacher of Christian doctrine. As if it were not bad enough that Lewis had to have written in the first place! Should be avoided like the plague.

Deity (n.): A word that is almost always spelled *Diety*.

Deism (n.): The doctrine that God exists but is too busy making clocks to interfere with the ongoing history of the world.

Demon (n.): A spiritual being whose primary function is to absolve human beings of responsibility for their problems. Anyone who questions this is obviously oppressed by a Spirit of Doubt.

Denial 1 (n.): A river in Egypt. Egyptian model rocket clubs are "either in Recovery or in Denial." 2 (n.): Normality.

Denomination (n.): An organized group of Christians differing from all other Christians. Those belonging to other denominations (see *Heretic*) are considered either pagans or (in the more enlightened groups) merely spiritually inferior, benighted, and disobedient Christians. Denominations differ over the precise method of baptism they use, the precise shade of Calvinism vs. Arminianism they embrace, the precise level of formality desired in their services, the precise kind of clothing their ministers wear, and/or simply which other denomination they split off from and at what period of history.

Derrida, Jacques (n.): *Post-Modernist* (q.v.) French philosopher and literary critic whose major theory, *Deconstruction* (q.v.), seems to have arisen from a need to maintain that all previous writers were actually, contrary to all appearances, as incomprehensible as he was.

> Derrida
> Is Post-Modernism's pa.
> He thinks that any wisdom which from the Ancients we have plucked
> Ought to be made to deconstruct.

Devil, The (n.): The head of the *Demons* (q.v.); he who, in a profound half truth, is blamed for the asininity of humankind.

Devil's Dictionary of the Christian Church, The, 2nd ed. Middletown, RI: Stone Tower Press, 2026 (n.): That which you are reading; the most brilliant piece of theological research from the beginning of the Twenty-First Century; that which you should buy innumerable copies of for all your friends and relatives.

Devotions, Personal (n.): A daily period of Bible reading, meditation, and prayer, usually neglected either upon first rising for the day or just before retiring for the evening; cf. *Quiet Time*.

Diaspora (n.): The state of having been scattered far and wide by persecution, as in the Jews during the exilic period, the Christians in the First Century, or the *Congregation's* (q.v.) wits during the *Sermon* (q.v.).

Dilbert (n.): Business consultant whose books describe the Church office, Denominational office, Mission Board home office, or Church College office even better than they do the secular marketplace.

Disciple 1 (n., archaic): A believer in Jesus as Lord who has been baptized in the name of the Father, the Son, and the Holy Spirit, and who is learning to do all things whatsoever Jesus has commanded him. 2 (n., current): Unknown. 2 (vb., trans., archaic): To recruit someone as a *disciple* (q.v.) and then be committed in an ongoing fashion to helping the recruit down that path (see def. 1). 4 (vb., trans., current): Unknown.

Disciples' Prayer, The. Camp Hill, PA: Christian Publications, 1999; reprinted by Wipf and Stock (n.): Pestiferous attempt by that annoying archaic wannabe *Donald T. Williams* (q.v.) to expound The Lord's Prayer as a model for praying Christians. Should be studiously avoided by anyone who wishes his clearly already perfectly adequate spiritual life to be undisturbed.

Discord 1 (n.): A sound frequently produced by the interactions between the *Piano* (q.v.) and the *Organ* (q.v.), the *Choir* (q.v.) and the *Accompaniment* (q.v.), or the *Sermon* (q.v.) and *Reason* (q.v.). 2 (n.): The opposite of dat cord.

Dispensationalism (n.): The doctrine that God dispensed with continuity in constructing his plan for the ages.

Disputation (n.): A formal debate about theology; the use of such benign spiritual gifts as *ad hominem*, red herring, begging the question, wrenching from context, the bandwagon appeal, poisoning the well, and shouting to edify the church by clarifying divine truth.

District Superintendent (n.): Denominational official who knows better than God or the *Congregation* (q.v.) where a given pastor should serve.

Divorce (n.): A social expedient which Christians condemn more than anybody else and practice just as much. Once committed, it becomes the Unpardonable Sin, unless one is a Media Personality. Then a period of mandatory penance, *Counseling* (q.v.), and rehabilitation is imposed: five minutes for popular recording artists, ten for media preachers. For preachers not blessed by the *Media* (q.v.), there is no reprieve.

Doctrinal Statement (n.): The *Confession of Faith* (q.v.) of a *Denomination* (q.v.) that does not believe in *Creeds* (q.v.) or *Confessions of Faith.*

Doctor of Divinity (n.): An honorary doctorate for those who barely finished *Bible College* (q.v.).

Documentary Hypothesis (n.): In *Biblical Criticism* (q.v.), the theory that, in a search for a more varied vocabulary, Moses created the Pentateuch as a hodge-podge from various sources such as J, E, P, D, Q, and *John Milton* (q.v.).

Doggerel (n.): The poetry found in *Sermons* (q.v.), denominational magazines, and church *Bulletins* (q.v.).

Dogmatic (adj.): Having a perverse, stubborn attachment to opinions or doctrines other than one's own.

Dogmatics (n.): The branch of theology that deals with canines.

Donation of Constantine (n.): Forged document allegedly by Constantine granting possession of the Vatican to the Papacy; part of the foundation of that institution's claims to authority. Since the papacy is infallible, of course it never *really* meant to claim that the document was genuine. See *Valla, Lorenzo*.

Donne, John (n.): Seventeenth-century figure who gave up a perfectly honorable career as a playboy and minor government official to become a *Preacher* (q.v.) and devotional poet.

Dordt, Canons of (n.): Heavy artillery used by *Calvinists* (q.v.) against their opponents.

> When, deep in the doctrinal fort,
> Our stockpile of prooftexts runs short,
> When we're feeling surrounded,
> By Heretics hounded,
> We fire the Canons of Dordt!

Doubt (v., t.): Sinfully and perversely to wonder whether things are really true when your only reason for believing them is that your parents or the *Preacher* (q.v.) said that they were so. DesCartes thought that doubt could function as a virtue, leaving one's true beliefs more certain as a result of the process; but he was obviously a Heretic and, what's worse, a Philosopher.

> There once was a man named DesCartes
> Who asked, "Where should Philosophy start?"
> He said, "If I can doubt it,
> I'll just do without it.
> Now, that ought to make me look smart!"

So he doubted the clear and the plain
To see what would finally remain.
    'Twas thus he found out
    There was no way to doubt
The doubt in the doubter's own brain.

"I exist!" then with joy he concluded.
"On this point I cannot be deluded:
    Even though it sounds dumb,
    If I think—*ergo sum*!"
To this day he has not been refuted.

If you ask what this tale is about,
It's that doubting must always run out.
    For you never can doubt
    That you're doubting the doubt
That you doubt when you're doubting your doubt.

E

Eagle and Child, The (n.): Cf. *Bird and Baby, The.*

Ecclesiology (n.): That branch of *Theology* (q.v.) which is ignored in all discussions of the nature, mission, and order of the church.

Ecumenical (adj.): Pertaining to the belief that Christians should agree to disagree about everything which divides them, since none of their doctrines mean anything anyway; pertaining to a movement whose purpose is to implement that belief.

Education (n.): That which causes Christian young people to lose their faith. If this does not work, sending them to *Seminary* (q.v.) will usually finish the job. Education is a necessary evil, of which one should acquire the least amount possible in order to maintain one's faith while still getting access to the job market.

Education, Christian (n.) An oxymoron. Cf. *College, Bible*; *College, Christian Liberal Arts*; etc.

Edwards, Jonathan (n.): Theologian who wrote profoundly about God's love but is mainly remembered for a sermon on His wrath.

Effusion (n.): A method of *Baptism* (q.v.); what *Theologians* (q.v.) call pouring. Though this method is practiced by a minority of groups, its proponents are quite effusive about it.

Egalitarianism (n.): The teaching that women are just like men, only better. Cf. *Complementatianism* and *Hierarchicalism*.

Elan Vital (n.): "The life force": a word used by those who wish to make the secular religion of naturalistic evolution feel less secular and more religious.

> Riding high on the Life Force's highest, triumphant wave,
> Precariously poised above its lowest trough;
> When first he saw things *thus*, his face grew grave,
> And Bergson shuddered, and coughed a nervous cough.

Elder (n.): In Presbyterianism, a functionary who sits on a Board whose primary purpose is to perpetuate itself.

Emergent (adj.): A movement which endeavors to refute the *Seeker-Sensitive* (q.v.) *Mega-Church* (q.v.) by applying its exact principles to a different class of non-seekers.

An Encouraging Thought: The Christian Worldview in the Writings of J. R. R. Tolkien. Cambridge, OH: Christian Publishing House, 2018. Annoying archaic wannabe *Donald T. Williams* (q.v.) makes those awful books by Tolkien even worse by explaining what they mean. Fans of Tolkien who wish to remain secure in their ignorance and misunderstanding should avoid this book at all costs!

End Times (n.): The Last Days; a period about which we know almost nothing except that it is coming; an illustration of the principle that the multiplication of verbiage is in inverse ratio to the amount of sure knowledge of the subject; therefore, a cash cow for the Christian Publishing Industry.

English (adj.): Belonging to the language of Heaven and the Edenic speech which survived the confusion of tongues at the Tower of Babel. This all follows from the fact that the original language of Scripture is that of the *King James* Version (q.v.). Unfortunately, certain corruptions of the original language of the Bible have occurred on both sides of the Atlantic since then.

"Whilst" instead of "while";
For "Excuse me," "Sorry!"
That's the British style:
A "truck" becomes a "lorry."
What we call a "conservative"
In England is a "Tory."
Americans "drop by"
While Brits "pop over to."
No one knows just why.
A "bathroom" is a "loo."
Americans have to "stand in line,"
While Englishmen just "queue."
We have a "can" for "trash";
They have a "bin" for "dust."
We're "knocked out" when we're bashed;
The English get "concussed."
They stay to leftward when they drive
To keep us all nonplussed.
Two nations thus divided
By a common tongue—
The rule by which we're guided
However far we're flung:
One of those things the gods decided
When the world was young.

English Civil War (n.): That period in history (the 1640's) when people who agreed that the Bible is the inspired Word of God, that Jesus was God in human flesh, that He died for our sins and was raised from the dead, and that salvation is offered by grace through faith in His name, nevertheless felt obliged to attack, burn out, starve, kill, and maim one another because they disagreed about the precise organization of church administration, how formal the service should be, and what kind of clothes the *Preacher* (q.v.) should wear.

Episcopalian (n.): One who believes that any religious or secular ideology whatsoever, even biblical Christianity, is compatible with the Thirty-Nine Articles.

Epistemology 1 (n.): In *Philosophy* (q.v.), the study of the nature, grounds, and limits of knowledge. Most (Post)-Modern thinkers have concluded that we can not know anything, but that most people do not know this, so they can get away with philosophizing anyway. 2 (n): Pistemology pursued on the Internet.

> "Our knowledge," one sage used to rant,
> "Is inevitably always aslant.
> The true Ding an Sich
> Is so sly and so slick
> That when you try to see it, you Kan't."

Epistle 1 (n.): The wife of an *Apostle* (q.v.); 2 (n.): a Pistle sent over the Internet.

> Paul the Apostle
> Was not exactly docile.
> He could fire off an epistle
> Like a guided missile.

Erasmus, Desiderius (n.): Renaissance scholar who discovered the *Original Greek* (q.v.) and edited his translation of the King James Bible for publication. He also laid an egg which was hatched by *Martin Luther* (q.v.) and wrote a book, *The Praise of Folly*, which had no influence whatsoever on this Dictionary.

Eschatology (n.): That branch of *Theology* (q.v.) which takes literally every biblical statement about the *End Times* (q.v.) except the one which says that it is impossible to figure out the Day or the Hour.

> Though it's something that Scripture berates,
> Still it keeps coming out of our pates:
>   We can't seem to resist
>   Much less cease or desist
> The incessant resetting of Dates.

Established (adj.): Referring to a *Denomination* (q.v.) which is officially recognized and supported by the State, which does this because it is a much more effective method than *Persecution* (q.v.) of rendering the Church impotent or destroying it.

Eternal (adj.): Having the characteristics of a period which, after an unladen swallow, making round trips from the Statue of Liberty to the Rock of Gibraltar and brushing the Rock once lightly with its wingtip on each circuit, and having thus finally worn the Rock completely away, would have just begun. Many questions remain about the Eternal: Is the swallow African or European? How does it live long enough to complete its task? Since it would need to eat during its trans-oceanic flight in order to sustain life and replenish energy for all those wingbeats, and would therefore have to carry food, how can it be unladen? Why does Eternity take so long to begin? Why does the swallow pursue such an inefficient method of wearing away the

Rock? Why does the swallow want to wear away the Rock in the first place? And what does the swallow do after that? But the answers are more than we can digest at the present time.

A scholar of divinity
Was studying eternity
And since he had a minute, he
Sat down to write a paper.
But e'er that he could pen it, he
Found that he must begin it; he
Met Despair, and in it, he
Got lost as in a vapor.
For eternity's infinity,
Though open to the Trinity,
To man's soul is a mystery
And always will escape her.
Well—if it seemed hard to begin it, he
Should have tried to *end* it! He
Would still this very minute be
A-working on that paper.

Eternity (n.): A popular Christian magazine of the 60's, 70's, and 80's which was intelligent, liked the present writer's work, and consequently came to an end.

Eucharist (n.): A fancy-schmancy word for *Communion* (q.v.); what *Theologians* (q.v.) call the Lord's Supper.

Evangelical 1 (n.): A *Fundamentalist* (q.v.) with a PhD—or at least any college education beyond a *Bible-College* (q.v.) certificate. Evangelicals differ from Fundamentalists in agreeing with Billy Graham that it is perfectly all right to send your converts to churches that do not believe the Bible, as long as they sincerely support your crusades. 2 (adj.): Having the characteristics of an Evangelical: flabby; wishy-washy; tacky.

Evangelism (n.): The *Sheep Stealing* (q.v.) practiced by one's own denomination.

Evangelistic (adj.): Having lots of Buses, Visitation Teams, and *Altar Calls* (q.v.).

Ex Cathedra (adv., Lat.): "On the throne"; the position from which the *Pope* (q.v.) produces the papal *Bull* (q.v.).

Exposition (n.): Obfuscation that proceeds verse by verse instead of topically.

Extend the Right Hand of Fellowship (v., t.): To shake hands; a ritual for welcoming new members, considered, as with prize fighters, an appropriate prelude to the first round of *Gossip* (q.v.) and Back-Stabbing.

F

Facebook (n.): A social medium which allows Christians to spread the Gospel and advance the Kingdom by posting pictures of their breakfasts and videos of their cats, and by expressing their contempt for and arguing interminably with anyone whose doctrinal or political choices differ from theirs by the merest jot or tittle. This is known as "speaking the truth in love."

Fact (n.): An assertion with which one agrees.

Fact, False (m.): An assertion with which one disagrees.

Fad (n.): The alternative to hidebound traditionalism.

Faith 1 (n., archaic): The art of continuing to believe what one knows on perfectly good grounds to be true in the face of appearances to the contrary. 2 (n., current): The inability of contrary evidence to register in the mind; or, if it does, an unnatural capacity for rationalization; considered a great *Virtue* (q.v.).

Faith, Living By (n.): An excuse not to pay the hired help a living wage.

Fallacy (n.): A specious argument. Fallacies are usually classified as Formal or Informal Fallacies; the difference is that Formal Fallacies are considered more appropriate for inclusion in the Sunday Morning *Sermon* (q.v.), while Informal Fallacies are reserved for the Evening Service.

Fellowship (n.): Church-speak for hanging out.

Fellowship Hall (n.): A large open area, often in the Church Basement, where gluttony is practiced when the weather is too inclement for the *Church Picnic* (q.v.).

Finney, Charles Grandison (n.): Nineteenth-Century Evangelist who invented the *Revival* (q.v., "current") and the *Altar Call* (q.v.), thereby relieving the Church of the embarrassment of having existed for eighteen centuries with no means of fulfilling its mission.

Five Points (n.): A summary of Calvinism by its enemies which *Calvinists* (q.v.) have adopted as their own—thus raising certain interesting questions about who their real theological enemies actually are.

Flame War (n.): The public shaming on social media of one who commits some horrible sin such as disagreement with oneself, membership in another *Denomination* (q.v.), or independent thought. Cf. *Burning at the Stake*; *Auto da Fe.*

Flesh, The (n.): The regrettable tendency of human beings to have bodies, with their attendant needs and appetites. The sins of the flesh, being gross and palpable, are far worse than those of the spirit, such as pride, self righteousness, etc., which are actually almost virtues.

Flowery (adj.): Characterized by overblown, grandiloquent, and/or excessively florid language; the angels would weep for very shame, sending their golden tears cascading through the saffron light of sunset, at the flowery diction in this definition; a tendency in certain practitioners of the *Sermon* (q.v.).

When the eloquence waxes ornate,
It's something the auditors hate.
    The whole congregation
    Just goes on vacation
And dreams of the roast on the plate.

Fortitude (n.): The ability to act pompously and arrogantly while safely ensconced inside one's protective fort; the ability to taunt one's opponents a second time.

Francis of Assisi, St. (n.): Medieval saint whose siblings included the Sun, the Moon, and an Ass. Escaping from this brilliant but monstrous family, he became a hermit and contemplative and founded the Franciscan order.

Free Will (n.): The capacity of human beings to make fools of themselves.

Freud, Sigmund (n.): The inventor of *Counseling* (q.v.) and creator of a number of theories and bits of jargon; but he was probably only dreaming.

Sigmund Freud
Grew very annoyed
When his superego tried to slam the lid
Down on his id.

Friar (n.): One of a medieval order of itinerant monks, so named for their devotion to a particular method of preparing capons for consumption.

Fundraising (n.): The ministry of parting fools from their money by using *argumentum ad populam, argumentum ad misericordiam*, and lots of wavy underlining.

Fundamentalist 1 (n.): One who sits on his fundament thinking up rules to follow, things to abstain from, and people to criticize for being less strict than he is. An alternative theory is that the word is related to the adj. *fundamental* and refers to certain doctrines considered essential to historic Christianity. But since no fundamentalist in the pew could be found who knew what these alleged doctrines were, this theory has no credibility. 2 (adj.): More *legalistic* (q.v.) than the speaker.

> I don't drink, smoke, cuss, or chew,
> And I don't go with girls that do.
> I won't play cards or watch a movie:
> I don't do *anything* that's groovy.

G

Gerl, Mark (n.): Archaic wannabe and therefore deservedly obscure Computer Geek, Educator, Youth Leader, and Sunday School Teacher who has no sense of humor whatsoever and did not write an Appendix to this Dictionary.

Gift, Spiritual 1 (n., archaic): An ability granted by God to the individual believer for the edification of the church; 2 (n., current, Pentecostal/Charismatic): *Speaking in Tongues* (q.v.); 3 (n., Baptist): *Tithing* (q.v.).

Glossolalia (n.): The gift of recreating the experience of the Tower of Babel. See *Tongues, Speaking in*.

Gnostic (n.): Heretic from the archaic period of Church History who believed that spirit was good and matter evil, and that salvation was for those who knew the secret codes. Kicked out the front door by the *Church Fathers* (q.v.), they have since sneaked back in through the back door disguised as *Fundamentalists* (q.v.).

Goat (n.): The *Sheep* (q.v.) which belong to another fold (cf. *Denomination*).

Gospel 1 (n., archaic): The Good News that God so loved the world that he gave his only begotten Son so that whosoever believeth in him should not perish, but have everlasting life; 2 (n., current): the good news that the nasty, judgmental God of the Old Testament has been sacked and replaced by Jesus, who is too busy running a Seminar on whether or not he actually said or did anything to worry about our sins; 3 (adj.): referring to a segment of the Country Music industry which replaces the words *beer*, *trucks*, and *cheatin'* with the words *white robes*, *golden streets*, and *Jesus*.

Gossip 1 (v., i.): To share prayer requests out of a wholly altruistic and disinterested concern for the wellbeing of one's fellow Christians. If others misuse the information we have passed on, or if it turns out to be inaccurate, we can hardly be blamed for that. 2 (n.): Prayer requests made on behalf of others without their knowledge or consent. After all, they might be too shy to ask.

Gothic (adj.): Pertaining to a style of church architecture employing pointy arches; often used in cathedrals as in keeping with the pointy hair of the bishops. See *Dilbert*, *Miter*.

Graham, Billy (n.): A scientific singularity; an anomaly; a Twentieth-Century Evangelist who utterly befuddled his followers, puzzled the press, confused the critics, frustrated the Fundamentalists, and perplexed the pundits by conducting a prominent media ministry for over half a century without the least hint of financial or sexual scandal.

Grammar (n.): That which only Intellectuals, English Professors, and other perverted deviants expect to be correctly used in the *Sermon* (q.v.) or the Freshman Paper.

> The student's paper, reeking red
> With ink, looked rather gory;
> Littered with the carcass of
> Another still-born story.

Another, of the Same
The student's paper, reeking red
With ink, looked rather messy,
Littered with the carcass of
Another still-born essay.

Great Awakening, The First (n.): That which occurs between the Morning Service and the Afternoon Nap.

Great Awakening, The Second (n.): That which occurs between the Evening Service and Bedtime.

Great Commandment, The 1 (n., archaic): To love the Lord your God with all your heart, soul, mind, and strength. 2 (n., current): To maintain a public image unspotted from the *World* (q.v.).

Great Commission, The 1 (n., archaic): The commandment that Christians go into all the world to make disciples; 2 (n., current): The commandment that Christians send Others into all the world to make converts; cf. *Missionary, Missions*.

Great Pumpkin, The (n.): He who rises out of the most sincere pumpkin patch in the land on the night of Halloween. Why he is not considered pagan and demonic, like having Witches as characters in the Narnia books, has never been adequately explained.

Greek, Original 1 (n.): An unknown descendant of Japheth and ancestor of Homer; erroneously thought to be the anonymous translator of the Bible into Greek from the original *King James* (q.v.), hence considered a great authority, as in the phrase, "according to the Original Greek ..." But as we now know that this was actually done by the Apostles, this theory has fallen into disrepute. 2 (n.): The language into which the Apostles translated the original *King James* (q.v.) so that the New Testament could be read in the First Century. As one of the earliest translations from the King James, the Greek text often provides great insight into its original meaning and hence much opportunity for *Preachers* (q.v.) to engage in obfuscation.

Greeter (n.): One of a legion of functionaries whose job is to pretend that they are regular members who would have been nice to you anyway.

Gregorian Chant (n.): A form of church music which is the polar opposite of *Contemporary Christian Music* (q.v.); i,e, it has melody without harmony or rhythm, as opposed to harmony and rhythm with no discernible melody.

Gregory the Great (n.): Pope who sent *Augustine of Canterbury* (q.v.) to evangelize angels. Due no doubt to a papal speech impediment, Augustine ended up in Britain evangelizing Angles and Saxons instead. In penance for this misunderstanding, Gregory abstained from all harmony and rhythm in church music and became the inventor of *Gregorian Chant* (q.v.).

Guilt (n.): Emotional distress, suffered over small, socially embarrassing offenses, which is sufficient to obscure those which are large and socially acceptable.

H

Half-Way Covenant (n.): The belief of some early New-England Puritans that, if the parents could be full members of the Church without being converted, then so could their children.

Health and Wealth (n.): That which flows from the gullible to the Televangelist. The temporal reward which naturally comes to those with the spiritual gifts of direct-mail fundraising, a charismatic personality, and a plentiful lack of conscience. That which they promise to their followers, who are obviously too spiritual to join the long line of humble, persecuted, suffering martyrs which constituted the membership of the Church in a more benighted age.

> Oh Lord, won't you give me a Mercedes Benz!
> My friends all have Porsches; I must make amends.
> I'm trying to cut back on most of my sins,
> So Lord, won't you give me a Mercedes Benz.
>
> (Apologies to Janis Joplin)

Heathen (n.): A member of a different *Denomination* (q.v.).

Heave Offering (n.): One of the possible results of combining gluttony with strenuous athletic activity. See *Church Picnic*.

Heaven (n.): The eternal abode of those like us; where we will live in everlasting bliss and harmony with those about whom we gossiped on earth.

Hebrew, Original 1 (n.): Abraham. 2 (n.): The language into which Moses and the prophets translated the original *King James* (q.v.) so that the Old-Testament saints could read the Bible. As one of the earliest translations from the King James, the Hebrew text often provides great insight into its original meaning and hence much opportunity for *Preachers* (q.v.) to engage in obfuscation.

Hell 1 (expl.): A bad word. 2 (n.): A place of eternal punishment reserved for pagans, infidels, intellectuals, and members of other *Denominations* (q.v.).

Henry, Carl F. H. (n.): *Theologian* (q.v.) and archaic wannabe who endeavored to refute the *Neo-Orthodoxy* (q.v.) of *Karl Barf* (q.v.) by writing a systematic theology that would be just as long and incomprehensible as the *Church Dogmatics*. Because he was writing in English rather than German, he failed on both counts.

Herbert, George (n.): Greatest Protestant devotional poet in history; hence utterly unknown in the contemporary church.

Heresy (n.): The doctrine held by one's ecclesiastical rivals.

Heretic (n.): Holding a different doctrinal position from the speaker, if the deviation is sufficiently serious to incur *Damnation* (q.v.). Otherwise the deviation is a mere doctrinal error and evidence not so much of perversity as mere denseness and stupidity. One of the primary ways of committing heresy is to differ from the speaker on the question of where the line is drawn between heresy and doctrinal error.

Heretical (adj.): In disagreement with the speaker.

Hermeneutics (n.): The science of interpretation; the art of making the Bible appear to support one's preconceived notions.

Hierarchicalism (n.): The teaching that men are supposed to treat women as Christ would, which obviously means bossing them around. Cf. *Complementarianism* and *Egalitarianism*.

Hismeneutics (n.): What *Hermeneutics* (q.v.) used to be called before the advent of gender-neutral language.

Hoc Est Corpus Meum (n.): The Latin phrase scrawled in chalk by *Martin Luther* (q.v.) on the conference table when he was discussing the *Eucharist* (q.v.) with *Zwingli* (q.v.) in the later stages of his career in vandalism. The Latin has been rendered "This is my body," but a more literal English translation would be "I'm more stubborn than you are, nyah, nyah, nyah!"

Holy (adj.): Tending to remind one of the style of worship, architecture, and life preferred by our *Denomination* (q.v.).

Holy Spirit (n.): That member of the Trinity who, in Pentecostal and Charismatic circles, replaces the other two, and who in almost all other circles is ignored completely.

Holy Spirit, Ministry of The (n.): A euphemism for emotional manipulation.

Homiletics (n.): The art of giving nonsense the illusion of organization by using volume and alliteration; three points and a poem.

> There once was a homiletician
> Who was bad about vain repetition.

Though he chose a new text,
His people were vexed
When the points were the same old edition.

Hope 1 (n., archaic): A vision of the future as dependent on God which enables one to persevere in the present. 2 (n., current): Wishful thinking.

Hume, David (n.): Eighteenth-Century philosopher who clearly proved that miracles are impossible because they can't happen.

David Hume
Would never presume
To credit a miracle;
He was much too empirical.

Humor, Sense of (n.): The ability to detect and appreciate irony, incongruity, wit, etc.; a personality trait rare among conservative Believers. The presence of it is usually sufficient to render the victim a misfit and outsider. As evidence, consider the prodigious number of people who are going to be grievously personally offended by this totally innocuous Dictionary.

Hymn (n.): A musical composition in which theologically intelligent praise is supposed to be addressed by the congregation to the Deity. However, as hymns are currently required to be mumbled at a dirge-like tempo accompanied by the unholy combination of droning organ and plinking piano, the original effect is usually sufficiently muffled.

Hymnbook (n.): A device for ruining the posture of Christians pretending to sing. These books are compiled by omitting at random fifteen of the twenty verses originally composed by the hymn writer, so that the *Song Leader* (q.v.) can then limit the verses actually sung to the first, second, and last of the five remaining—this being the only attempt at leadership in which he will actually be followed.

Hypocrisy (n.): The difference between what one says to the *Preacher* (q.v.) when shaking his hand on the way out of church, and what one says five minutes later.

I

Icon (n.): A cartoon drawing of the Trinity, Jesus, the virgin Mary, or a saint that is venerated in Roman Catholic or Eastern Orthodox worship practices. Veneration differs from worship in that it is claimed to be distinct from it, in ways more subtle than those in which a quacking and waddling aquatic avian differs from a duck. Protestant Evangelicals and Fundamentalists object to the gross idolatry of bowing before images; they prefer more subtle and abstract idols, such as money, sex, or political power.

Idea (n.): A distraction from the godly emotions which are the sole focus of worship and Christian instruction.

Idol (n.): What one worships in place of God, such as one's self, one's denomination, one's theology, or one's political party.

Illustration (n.): In the *Sermon*, (q.v.), a narrative rabbit trail which distracts the congregation from the absence of points.

Imagination (n.): A capacity which Satan sneaked into human nature while God wasn't looking; hence, like *Intellect* (q.v.), one which can only be used for evil.

Immersion (n.): A method of *Baptism* (q.v.); what *Theologians* (q.v.) call dunking (cf. *Effusion* and *Spargation*); while Baptists consider this a deep subject, other *Denominations* (q.v.) consider them to be all wet.

In Error (adj.): In disagreement with the speaker; cf. *heretical.*

Inclusive (adj.): Unable or unwilling to make or apply distinctions, as between genders in language or Christians and Pagans in *Members* (q.v.).

Indulgence 1 (n.): The third trip to the food table at the *Potluck Dinner* (q.v.); 2 (n.): A certificate granting absolution of sin, or remittance of time in *Purgatory* (q.v.) in exchange for the payment of money. The *Reformation* (q.v.) was precipitated when *Martin Luther* (q.v.) indulged himself in doubts over the propriety of this practice; the Pope's tolerance for indulging theological debate was exceeded when, as a result, sales went down. And the reader's capacity to indulge the author's propensity for indulging himself in the repetition of this particular pun was probably exceeded about a sentence ago.

Inerrancy (n.): The quality of being absolutely truthful and trustworthy, i.e., "without error"; ascribed by Roman Catholics to the Pope, by Conservative Protestants to the original manuscripts of the Bible, and by Liberal Protestants to the biblical *Critic* (q.v.).

Infallible (adj.): Not liable to lead one astray. Conservative *Protestants* (q.v.) attribute this quality to Scripture, Roman *Catholics* (q.v.) to the *Pope* (q.v.), and *Liberals* (q.v.) to the *Biblical Critic* (q.v.).

Infinitive (n.): *To* plus a *verb*; that which one should not split. *To* unnecessarily, egregiously, grievously, shamefully, inexcusably, and without due cause *split* an infinitive could result in awkward sentence construction, which heaven forbid we should have in the *Sermon* (q.v.).

Inklings, The (n.): Group of Oxford eggheads who hung around with *C. S. Lewis* (q.v.) and corrupted the Christian faith by intellectualizing it. That they were Of the Devil is clearly shown by the fact that they smoked pipes, drank beer, met in a pub, and wrote books with witches and wizards in them.

Inklings II (n.): The writers' and artists' support group of Trinity Fellowship Evangelical Free Church of Toccoa, Georgia, which continues in existence after the dissolution of the church. That they are shady characters and probably deserve to be burned at the stake as heretics is plain from the fact that they attempt to commit the *Arts* (q.v.) and named themselves after the original *Inklings* (q.v.).

Inklings of Reality: Essays toward a Christian Philosophy of Letters, 2nd ed. Lantern Hollow Press, 2012. Stubborn attempt by that archaic wannabe *Donald T. Williams* (q.v.) to foster a healthy culture of faithful reading among Christians. *Under no circumstances* should this book be read by lovers of literature, English majors, Christian educators, home-schooling parents, or anyone else!

Innocence (n.): That which is lost by any contact with the Real World.

Intellect (n., archaic): The ability to think rationally and speak articulately; that God-given faculty which separates us from the animals and unites us to God. 2 (n., current): The only faculty of human beings which is so fallen that God cannot use it, Christ cannot redeem it, and the Holy Spirit cannot sanctify it. The only legitimate purpose it serves is that of thinking up clever arguments against its own use.

Intellectual 1 (n.): A person who willfully and maliciously uses the *Intellect* (q.v.) for illegitimate purposes such as questioning, analysis, creativity, etc., and is even perverse enough to enjoy it. Highly susceptible to such pernicious influences as *Philosophy* (q. v.), *Theology* (q. v.), and the *Arts* (q. v.), intellectuals must be watched carefully and squelched at every opportunity lest they succeed, like *Socrates* (q. v.), in corrupting the youth. 2 (adj.): Having the characteristics of an *Intellectual* (sense 1); addicted to ideas, thinking, and other dangerous substances.

Intelligent (adj.): Unspiritual.

Interpretation (n.): See *Hermeneutics.*

Interregnum (n.): That period in history (the 1650's) when conservative Protestants, at the apogee of their influence, set up a *Theocracy* (q.v.) and thereby did us the favor of insuring that they would never be permitted to do so again. Cf. *Protectorat*e.

Introduction 1 (n.): A brief oration warning the *Congregation* (q.v.) of the imminent appearance of the Special Speaker so that they can begin settling in for a long winter's nap. It usually consists of a summary of his life and accomplishments and the threat that he will attempt to bless the Congregation's hearts. 2 (n.): That part of the *Sermon* (q.v.) in which the *Preacher* (q.v.) chattily ingratiates himself with the *Congregation* (q.v.), announces his *Text* (q.v.), and botches the obligatory *Joke* (q.v.), a comforting ritual which allows the auditory to complete the process of settling in for that long winter's nap.

Invitation (n.): The part of the *Altar Call* (q.v.) in which people are exhorted to make a public confession of Christ while every head is bowed and every eye closed.

Invocation (n.): The moment which divides *Gossip* (q.v.) from Sleep.

Irony (n.): That which those who are offended by the totally innocent form of light entertainment currently before them are obviously incapable of perceiving, understanding, or appreciating.

J

Jargon (n.): The native speech of Theologians, Philosophers, and Literary Critics. Like *Glossolalia* (q.v.), a pristine language surviving unchanged by time from the Tower of Babel.

Joke (n.): In the *Sermon* (q.v.), an effort by the *Preacher* (q.v.) to ingratiate himself with the *Congregation* (q.v.); the obligatory waking up of the *Congregation* at the beginning of the *Sermon* so they can take their sleeping pill.

Judgment, Day of (n.): the *Parousia* (q.v.) as it will be experienced by the Wicked, i.e., those in other *Denominations* (q.v.).

Judgmental (adj.): Critical of oneself, or of the scams, schuysters, and mountebanks which one currently supports or favors.

Justice (n.): That which favors our interests or those of the groups to which we belong.

Justification (n.): A word which is used to convey the false impression that one understands something about *Salvation* (q.v.); for *Protestants* (q.v.), the removal of one's *Sins* (q.v.) so that one can start fresh on another round; for *Catholics* (q.v.), being finally forgiven after several thousand years in *Purgatory* (q.v.).

K

Kenosis (n.): A word *Theologians* (q.v.) use to avoid communicating the idea that Jesus humbled Himself in the Incarnation.

Kerygma (n.): What theologians call the *Gospel* (q.v.); the good news that the nasty, judgmental God of the Old Testament has been sacked and replaced by Jesus, who is too busy running a Seminar on whether or not he actually said or did anything to worry about our sins.

King James Version (n.): The original text of Scripture, handed down by God to Adam and Eve in the Garden of Eden on tablets of gold. The Hebrew and Greek texts were translated from the original King James.

Kingdom (adj.): Pertaining to any of those motives, goals, activities, or policies favored by the speaker; as in the phrase "kingdom perspectives."

L

Laity (n.): Those *Members* (q.v.) who are not *Clergy* (q.v.). So named for the function they were designed to perform, i.e., *lay*ing bills in the *Collection* (q.v.) plate.

Late-Comers (n.): The congregation.

Latin (n.): The official language of ancient pagans, medieval theologians, and modern lawyers.

Legalism (n.): The doctrine that salvation is by grace alone apart from works and that the Ceremonial Law has been abrogated as obsolete, and it is therefore obviously our obligation to create a new Ceremonial Law of our own for people to follow if they want to be considered *spiritual* (q.v.).

Legalist (n.): One who abstains from more things, more loudly, than the speaker.

Lent (n.): That part of the Church Year, leading up to Holy Week, which is devoted to fasting and repentance; so named for the material normally removed after an extended period of navel-gazing.

Lewis, C. S.: Popularizer of Christian doctrine whose books, written for uneducated British citizens during World War II, are now considered to be impossibly intellectual.

Lexicographer (n.): One who writes Dictionaries; according to Dr. Johnson, "a harmless drudge." It takes one to know one.

License (n.): The libertinism practiced by others. When it is practiced by ourselves, it is known as "Christian liberty."

License, Poetic (n.): Permission given to poets to abuse the rules of grammar and sense with impunity. When conferred on *Preachers* (q.v.), it is known as *Ordination* (q.v.).

Liberal 1 (n.): One who believes that Jesus never said most of the words or did any of the deeds attributed to him, but that, for some reason which remains unclear, we should follow Him anyway. 2 (adj.): Having the characteristics of a liberal, i.e., learned but confused and confusing; most dangerous when attempting to do good.

Liberalism (n.): The belief that Jesus was either (a) a Nineteenth Century Rationalist Optimist Humanist, (b) a Twentieth Century Marxist Revolutionary, or (c) a Passivist Buddhist Pacifist (take your pick) before his time, but the Disciples created the myth of his miracles and resurrection as a distraction to cover their embarrassment at not having recognized this. Meanwhile, Paul transformed the Simple Religion of Jesus into the Roman Catholic Church while nobody was looking.

Lymerick (n.): A verse form consisting of five lines rhyming AABBA, with the A's in trimeter, the B's in dimeter; used primarily for humor and satire; therefore obviously having no place in this Dictionary.

> The list of words rhyming with *lymerick*
> Is little, it's short, and it's slimerick.
> But if you can't find it,

    Your readers won't mind it
As long as you give them a glimmerick.

There once was a lymerick writer
Whose income grew tighter and tighter.
    "If I want to make bread
    With my verses," he said,
"I will just have to be even snider."

A writer of verse from Hong Kong
Got all of his lymericks wrong.
    They started out fine
    From the very first line,
But the last one was almost always invariably and
without fail too long.

There was once a young writer of verse
Whose lines grew increasingly worse.
    He read them aloud
    To a violent crowd
And was driven away in a hearse.

Liturgical (adj.): Tending to plan one's *Service* (q.v.) according to the patterns of ancient *Tradition* (q.v.) rather than either making it up as one goes along or planning it according to the patterns of more modern forms of recreation; i.e., taking Rome or Canterbury, rather than Nashville or Hollywood, as the model for one's entertainments.

Liturgy (n.): Rigmarole, hoopla, and folderol that has actually been planned as opposed to made up on the spot "as the Spirit moves." See *Service*.

Lord's Day (n.): The last day of the weekend, i.e., Sunday, set aside by the faithful for the religious observances of going to church, taking naps, and watching football.

Lord's Prayer (n.): A short passage of Scripture which can be recited in lieu of an actual attempt to *Pray* (q.v.).

Lord's Supper (n.): A ritual meal of crackers and grape juice, which many churches continue out of habit to serve once a month, even though they have long since begun providing the superior refreshment of coffee and donuts every week.

Lordship Salvation (n.): The doctrine, obviously heretical, that Jesus Christ is Lord.

Lost 1 (adj.): Not saved, i.e., belonging to no church, or, worse, one in another *Denomination* (q.v.); 2 (n.): Those to whom the adjective applies.

Lucifer (n.): The true hero of both the Bible and *Paradise Lost*; his beneficent role in the liberation of humankind was suppressed by the Roman Catholic Church when it rewrote the Bible to eliminate all references to Jesus' marriage to *Mary Magdalene* (q.v.); cf. *Satan*.

Lust (n.): The worst of the *Seven Deadly Sins* (q.v.); the only one of them that Protestants actually preach against. As for practicing it ...

Before he was saved, St. Augustine
Was in love with the pleasure of lustin'.
He prayed, "Make me pure,
But not *yet*, to be sure!"
While he prayed, his own prayer he was bustin'.

Luther, Martin (n.): Late medieval monk who was excommunicated on charges of vandalism relating to a certain incident involving a Door in Wittenberg in 1517, when he unwittingly started the *Reformation* (q.v.).

> Brother Martin
> Left the Papacy smartin'.
> He caused a sensation
> By starting the Reformation.

Lutheran (n.): A member of the *Denomination* (q.v.) featured on "The Prairie Home Companion"; one who wishes to avoid Good Works in order to be saved.

M

Magdalene, Mary (n.): The wife of Jesus. This obvious fact was violently suppressed by the Roman Catholic Church on the wholly specious and inadequate grounds that it was only mentioned by late and apocryphal writers and the original eyewitnesses seemed unaware of it.

Magi (n.): The pagan wizards and astrologers ("Wise Men"), traditionally three in number, who visited the infant Christ in the manger. Why their presence in the narrative has not caused the Gospel of Matthew to be condemned as satanic for promoting witchcraft like the Narnia books has never been adequately explained.

Magisterium (n.): The teaching authority of the Roman Catholic Church, so named because it consists of a number of *Magi*, or allegedly wise men, trying to *steer* the Church along the path of orthodoxy. An alternative explanation is that the *steer* is related to the same beasts that produce the papal *Bull* (q.v.)

Majority (n.): The number of hands that the Chair sees, or voices that he hears, when he favors the motion being voted on in the *Church Business Meeting* (q.v.).

Majority Text (n.): In textual criticism, the theory that the more times a scribal error is copied, the more authoritative it becomes.

Mammon (n.): An ancient deity unfairly frowned upon by the biblical writers but much worshiped by contemporary believers; cf. *Heath and Wealth*.

Margin (n.): That portion of *Scripture* (q.v.) which is reserved for explanatory comments, doodles, and notes to one's fellow sufferers in the *Service* (q.v.).

Marriage (n.): *Purgatory* (q.v.).

Martyr (n.): One who voluntarily forgoes his morning nap and stays awake for the duration of the *Sermon* (q.v.).

Marx, Karl (n.): A member of the Marx brothers who was banned from the group by Groucho, Harpo, and Chico for having no sense of humor. In retaliation, he proved them right by writing the *Communist Manifesto*.

Mask (n.): That which was for most of history a sign of evil intent, but which in 2020 became the sign of a law-abiding and public-spirited citizen; a versatile device which allows both those who wear it and those who do not to engage in virtue signaling—sold, of course, for the prevention of disease only.

Mass Production (n.): The process of pulling off Roman Catholic worship services.

Media (n.): That word which, when singular, is condemned by Scripture as occultic, but which, when plural, becomes the true god of popular Evangelicalism, whose blessing overcomes every shortcoming and absolves of all evil.

Meek (adj.): Able to listen to preachers, theologians, and denominational officials with a humble mien and a straight face.

Mega-Church (n.): A *Denomination* (q.v.), all of the members of which meet for church in the same shopping mall.

Member (n.): One of the individuals who allegedly make up the roster of a given congregation. Less than one half of them can usually be found or accounted for.

Meme (n.): The Protestant alternative to the *Icon* (q.v.). An obnoxiously aggressive (Fundamentalists) or sentimental (Evangelicals) picture carrying alleged spiritual symbolism and distributed across the Internet in lieu of conducting actual personal evangelism.

Mercy (n.): The attitude which others should show to our failings and shortcomings.

Mere Humanity: G. K. Chesterton, C. S. Lewis, and J. R. Tolkien on the Human Condition, 2ne ed. Chillicothe, OH: DeWard, 2018 (n.): Recalcitrant attack on reductionism and defense of a biblical view of human nature by that irritating archaic wannabe *Donald T. Williams* (q.v.) that is almost as bad as the other authors it purports to study.

Merit (n.): Credits which can be cashed in, by *Protestants* (q.v.) for *Salvation* (q.v.), or by *Catholics* (q.v.) for released time from *Purgatory* (q.v.). They can be earned by *Attendance* (q.v.), *Tithing* (q.v.), or *Abstinence* (q.v.).

Messiah, The (n.): The only piece of classical music which is allowable to perform in Church, but then no more than once a year and only in a severely expurgated version consisting mostly of the "Hallelujah Chorus." All of which is very strange, seeing that Christians were originally against having it performed at all.

The pious found a way to be offended.
God's Word sung in a public Music Hall!
It truly was a venue to appall,
Incapable of being comprehended.
Why, vulgar entertainments there were vended,
With doors thrown open wide to one and all.
To mix the Gospel with such folderol?
An error that could hardly be amended.

And what would these blasphemers think of next,
So careless of the Church's reputation?
Why not associate with sinners? Why,
You might as well proclaim the sacred Text
Of God's pure kingdom and His great salvation
Out on a hillside underneath the sky.

Messianic Secret (n.): Shhh! Not so loud!

Methodist (n.): One who believes that the best way to honor the memory of *John Wesley* (q.v.) is to deny or ignore everything he stood for; conversely, one who does not believe this, but thinks that the best way to honor John Wesley is to belong to a *Denomination* (q.v.) which does.

Middle Knowledge (n.): The doctrine of *Luis de Molina* (q.v.) that knowing everything is only a middling kind of *Omniscience* (q.v.), for which God compensates by also knowing things that are not necessarily so, but could be.

Millennial (n.): A member of that generation whose existence probably is a sign of the End Times. To be distinguished from Pre-Millennials (i.e., Baby Boomers), Post-Millennials (i.e., infants), and A-Millennials (those who do not identify with any generation).

Millennium (n.): A period of 1,000 years which either will or will not occur either before or after the Second Coming of Christ; cf. *Parousia, Eschatology*.

Milton, John (n.): English poet whose *Paradise Lost*, an account of the creation and fall of Man, was allegedly, according to one theory, used as a source by Moses in the composition of the Pentateuch (cf. *Criticism, Biblical* and *Documentary Hypothesis*). But since we now know that the Pentateuch was merely translated into Hebrew by Moses from the original *King James* (q.v.), this theory has no credibility.

Minister 1 (v., i.): To attempt to trick the congregation into believing that they have been edified; i.e., to palm off as entertainment that which would not be accepted as such without the use of the word, as in the phrase "minister in song." 2 (n.): A *Preacher* (q.v.) with pretensions to dignity and decorum.

Ministry (n.): A generic term for any type of religious work or for an organization whose ostensible purpose is to perform such; used to grant an aura of dignity to inferior entertainment or to justify the failure to pay a living wage.

Mission Trip (n.): An admirable device which allows one to take a vacation to an exotic location and gain spiritual brownie points at the same time. In order to earn the points, one must undergo some major suffering, such as drinking bottled water or enduring a bout of jet lag.

A good definition of pain
Is the agony, suffering, and strain
You inflict on your knee
When you force it to be
Between two coach seats on a plane.

Missionary (n.): One who is compensated for living in huts and eating bugs by getting to make slide presentations in the Evening Service.

Missions (n.): An enterprise fueled by the fact that it is less threatening to pay someone else to take the Gospel across an ocean by proxy than it is to take it across the street yourself.

Miter (n.): Ecclesiastical headgear worn by *Bishops* (q.v.) to hide their pointy hair. See *Dilbert*.

Mitosis (n.): Cell division, eventuating in two complete new organisms; a form of reproduction favored by the Church; cf. *Church Split*.

Moderation (n.): The virtue of doing things to the same extent or with the same fervor that we do, as opposed to the extremes of more or less practiced by others.

Modernism (n.): The belief that we know more than our ancestors did because we have learned how to perform neat parlor tricks with matter. When applied to religion, this attitude produces classical *Liberalism* (q.v.). After a gestation period of a couple of centuries or so, it gives birth to *Post-Modernism* (q.v.), which will no doubt lead to Post-Post-Modernism if it doesn't deconstruct first.

Molina, Luis de (n.): Renaissance *Theologian* (q.v.) who taught that God knows things that ain't so, but which would be so if they were so. God then arranges the Circumstances so that the things that He knows are going to be so will be so. This arranging of Circumstances is a form of "meddling" with people's free will, which, due to poor spelling, became known as *Middle Knowledge* (q.v.).

Monasticism (n.): That movement which vows to practice poverty, chastity, and obedience. In its early days it sometimes did, while preserving the Bible and Western Civilization in its spare time. In later times, various forms of monkey business ensued.

Money Changers (n.): An older designation for the Church Treasurer.

Monk (n.): The life-long inmate of a certain type of ecclesiastical prison, to which he was sent for monkeying around.

Moody, Dwight L. (n.): Nineteenth-century shoe salesman who, in his spare time, produced numerous sermons, altar calls, and sound bytes, along with a college, a church, a magazine, and a long beard.

More, Thomas (n.): Sixteenth-century lawyer and politician who served as Lord Chancellor of England under Henry VIII, wrote *Utopia*, and lost his head over the *Act of Supremacy* (q.v.).

Motivation (n.): Guilt.

Muses, the Nine (n.): Pagan wenches in charge of the *Arts* (q.v.). They were false gods and probably witches too. The conclusion is inevitable.

N

Name it and Claim it (v., t.): Blab it and Grab it. See *Health and Wealth.*

Nave (n.): That part of the *Sanctuary* (q.v.) where the knaves stand or sit during the *Service* (q.v.).

Nazi 1 (n., archaic): A member of the National Socialist Party which ruled Germany during World War II and perpetrated the Holocaust against Jews; 2 (n., current): Any person of whose politics the speaker disapproves.

Neo-Orthodox (adj.): Neither orthodox nor heretical. The first two letters appear to be from the word *neither*, with an *o* inserted for euphony. Fundamentalists and Evangelicals believe that Jesus rose bodily and literally from the dead. Liberals believe that the spirit of Christ triumphed over the disciples' despair, but that Jesus himself stayed dead as a doornail. The Neo-Orthodox believe that Jesus sort of rose from the dead, in his body, kind of, in history, more or less.

Neo-Orthodoxy (n.): The system of contradictory premises (the Bible is full of myths and errors but is the Word of God anyway; Jesus rose from the dead, but not in regular history open to verification) somehow swallowed by the Neo-Orthodox.

Newman, John Henry (n.): Nineteenth-Century cleric who invented the *Tract* (q.v.), had an idea for a university, converted to *Roman Catholicism* (q.v.), and played for the *Cardinals* (q.v.), but later apologized for his whole life.

News, Fake (n.): Any report which disagrees with, or does not seem sufficiently to favor, the reader or viewer's opinions, biases, or prejudices.

Newton, John (n.): Eighteenth Century religious figure who left a perfectly respectable career as a slave trader to become a disreputable Preacher and Hymn Writer; especially known for writing "Amazing Grace" and encouraging *William Wilberforce* (q.v.) to impose his personal values and religious beliefs on Parliament by abolishing the slave trade.

Nicaea, Council of (n.): Meeting of *Church Fathers* (q.v.) in 325 BC to obfuscate Christian teaching by accurately and succinctly summarizing what the Bible says about God and Jesus. Pay no attention to *Credo: Meditations on the Nicene Creed,* in which archaic wannabe *Donald T. Williams* (q.v.) tries to elucidate and apply its meaning for today; reading this book can only have the effect of deepening your spiritual life and putting you completely out of step with contemporary Christendom.

Nicholas, Saint (n.): Early church father who gave gifts to children and punched out Heretics (q.v.). Due to a triumphant public relations campaign, he is only remembered for one of those accomplishments.

Nietzsche, Friedrich (n.): Nineteenth-century *Philosopher* (q.v.) and writer who was the father of Nazism, Nihilism, and Post-Modernism, and who wrote Superman Comics. Actually, he claimed to be Superman himself, but kryptonite not having been discovered yet, it was impossible to test this claim.

Friedrich Nietzsche
Could often be preachy:
He thought the Will to Power
The need of the hour.

Ninety-Five Theses (n.): Pestilential document nailed to the Wittenberg Church Door in 1517 by *Martin Luther* (q.v.), who had nothing better to do than protest the sale of Salvation (q.v.) for money. The Protestant *Reformation* (q.v.) resulted from this act of ecclesiastical vandalism.

Ninety-Five Theses for a New Reformation: A Road Map for Post-Evangelical Christianity. *Semper Reformanda* Publications, 2021. Utterly futile attempt by that nasty archaic wannabe *Donald T. Williams* (q.v.) to start a new *Reformation* (q.v.)—or restart the first one. As if the original Reformation had not caused enough trouble!

Nunnery (n.): A convent; Ophelia willfully drowned herself to avoid going to one.

Nursery (n.): A holding cell for the incarceration of infants and toddlers during the *Service* (q.v.), so that their parents can sleep.

O

Ockham, William of (n.): Scholastic *theologian* (q.v.), favored by some Protestant Fundamentalists despite the fact that he was a philosopher (see *Philosophy*), because he can be read to have taught that one should not have any more thoughts than one can help.

> When superfluous thoughts troubled Ockham
> Like tails wagging dogs just to mock him,
>   He whipped out his razor,
>   As sharp as a laser,
> And calmly proceeded to dock 'em.

Offering (n.): The passing of the Plate so that the members may pretend to *Tithe* (q.v.).

Offertory (n.): The use of music to soothe the savage breasts of those sheep being subjected to the attempted fleecing known as the *Offering* (q.v.); it usually consists of the pianist hiding a hymn tune beneath various irrelevant and pretentious runs and arpeggios.

Omnipotence (n.): God's ability to make a stone so big He can't lift it, draw a square circle, and enable the Boston Red Sox and the Chicago Cubs to win the World Series.

Omniscience (n.): God's ability to keep a Naughty List by seeing you when you are sleeping and knowing when you are awake; delegated to *Saint Nicholas* (q.v.).

Ontological Argument (n.): An argument for the existence of God propounded by *Anselm of Canterbury* (q.v.). God is that being greater than which none can be conceived. If He didn't exist, He wouldn't be all that great, now, would He? Argal, Q. E. D. Some archaic Christians think the real argument isn't quite that silly, but, being philosophically minded, they are probably guilty of *Thought* (q.v.) and so should be discounted.

Orchestration (n.): The art of turning a simple and expressive hymn tune into something pretentious and bombastic.

Ordinances (n.): That which churches which do not practice the *Sacraments* (q.v.) call the *Sacraments*; e.g., the *Lord's Supper* (q.v.) served with grape juice instead of wine.

Ordination (n.): Being set aside for ministry by the laying on of the hands of the presbytery. If that does not work, it can be attempted again while the hands are holding blunt objects, sharp instruments, and whips.

Organ (n.): One of the two instruments (cf. *Piano*) handed down by God to Adam and Eve in the Garden of Eden, on which all church music must be played.

Orthodox 1 (adj., archaic): Holding correct doctrine. This meaning, along with its referent, seems to be passing out of usage. 2 (adj.): Catholic without the Pope, the lack of which is made up for by having more icons, more incense, and a more incomprehensible theology.

Oxymoron (n.): A rhetorical device, invented by a sophomore at Oxford University, in which opposite qualities are combined for effect, as in beloved enemy, cold fire, military intelligence, honest merchant, Church unity, Christian mind, etc.

P

Pabulum (n.): That which is fed literally to the babies in the *Nursery* (q.v.) and figuratively to the adults in the *Sermon* (q.v.).

Padding (n.): That which the *Pew* (q.v.) has in common with the *Sermon* (q.v.); optional for the *Pew*.

Pagan 1 (n., archaic): One who worships a false God; 2 (n., current): One who is on a different "page" from the speaker; 3 (adj.): Having the characteristics of a pagan.

Page (n.): That part of the *Hymnal* (q.v.) which is idly turned by those unable to get to sleep during the *Sermon* (q.v.).

Pandemic (n.): A public health crisis which requires people to stay home and practice *social distancing* (q.v.) unless they are engaged in rioting, looting, arson, or other forms of peaceful protest.

Parable (n.): A story used by Jesus to teach the people and confuse the *Theologians* (q.v.).

Paraclete (n.): That which those who wish to pretend they know Greek call the Holy Spirit.

Paradox (n.): More than one doc but fewer than three; i.e., two doctors of the Church who disagree with each other but, for the sake of Church unity, are both held to be right.

Parousia (n.): An attempt to avoid communication; what *Theologians* (q.v.) call the Second Coming (see *Eschatology*).

Pascal, Blaise (n.): French intellectual who lost all his credibility with modern Evangelicals when he was caught playing cards.

> There is a Pascal, name of Blaise,
> Who has a great game that he plays.
> "I'll make you a Wager:
> Now, which would be sager?
> God is; He is not. Which one pays?

Passage (n.): A portion of Scripture over which the eyes "pass" while disconnected from the brain during Bible reading. Cf. *Pericope*.

Pastor (n.): According to H. L. Mencken, "One employed by the wicked to prove to them by his example that virtue doesn't pay." What *Evangelicals* (q.v.) tend to call the functionary known by *Fundamentalists* (q.v.) as a *Preacher* (q.v.).

Pastoral Search Committee (n.): A group charged with producing a *Candidate* (q.v.) to fill a pastoral vacancy. They do this by looking for a man who is the Husband of one Wife (who must play the piano and have a perfect marriage without ever seeing her husband), who is twenty-five years old and has thirty years of experience, and who can preach challenging, prophetic sermons with which everyone in the *Congregation* (q.v.) will be completely comfortable.

Peace (n.): A state of emotional ease (cf. *comfortable*) used by the pious as a justification for any action or inaction, as in the sentence, "I have/do not have *peace* about that." Scripture is used to provide external support for decisions already reached on this basis. See *Prooftext*.

Pelagius (n.): Ancient theologian who denied the doctrine of original sin. Because he thought all our sins flowed from following Adam's example rather than from inheriting his nature, this meant that our sins are really only copies and not original at all. This view was modified by his son, *Semi-Pelagius* (q.v.), who sought a compromise with orthodoxy.

Perdition (n.): What *Theologians* (q.v.) call being *Lost* (q.v.). All human beings are subject to perdition unless redeemed by Christ: women because they cannot read maps, and men because they refuse to ask for directions.

Performance Tape (n.): Ecclesiastical karaoke; cf. *Special Music*.

Pericope (n.): A bit, piece, section, fragment, or chunk of Scripture; what *Theologians* (q.v.) call a *Passage* (q.v.).

Persecution 1 (n., American): Not being given preferential treatment. 2 (n., other): The act of making the Church stronger by trying to destroy it.

Person and Work of the Holy Spirit, The. Nashville: Broadman, 1994; reprinted by Wipf and Stock (n.): Heretical attempt by insufferable archaic wannabe *Donald T. Williams* (q.v.) to explain the entire work of the Holy Spirit as having the purpose of glorifying God the Son, on the specious grounds that Jesus said that is what is is. Should be avoided by anyone with any interest in sound theology, inspiration, illumination, conviction, calling, regeneration, spiritual gifts, or any number of other pestilential disasters lying in the path of comfortable religion.

Personally (adv.): Having no force or validity or tendency to be put into practice or any other meaning, as in the phrase, "While I'm *personally* opposed to abortion ...."

Pew (n.): A device for overcoming the sleep-inducing effects of the *Sermon* (q.v.) by rendering the victim extremely uncomfortable. There has been a long debate in the Church over whether sleeping or wakefulness is more desirable in the Congregation, for while awakening is a natural symbol of the Resurrection, sleep speaks eloquently of the Sabbath Rest. In a rare compromise accepted by most of Christendom, the claims of both states are recognized by combining the natural effects of the sermon with those of the pew and letting the congregation fall where they may.

> If slumber is what you pursue,
> There's really not much you can do
>   For your poor nodding head
>   When you're far from your bed
> And sitting upright in a pew.

Philosopher (n.): One who practices *Philosophy* (q.v.); a professional obfuscator and maker of the worse to appear the better reason; one who attempts to make *Theology* (q.v.) even more incomprehensible and confusing than it already is.

Philosophize (v., i.): Perniciously, irresponsibly, and with malice aforethought to commit the inexcusable, unforgivable, and mortal sin of *Thought* (q.v.). Normally cause for immediate shunning and excommunication.

Philosophy (n.): A form of intellectual combat whose object is to befuddle one's opponents into submission. Formerly, this was done by conducting all discussions in *Latin* (q.v.); but it has since been discovered that symbolic logic has an even greater obfuscatory power. Like *Theology* (q.v.), only worse.

If a tree in the forest falls down
When no one with ears is around,
Though it crashes like thunder,
Philosophers wonder
Whether there's really a sound.

Or else, when you exit a room,
Is it logical then to presume
That the Table or Chair
That you left is still there
Until your sensations resume?

Bishop Berkeley set briskly about
Proving beyond any doubt
That the Table and Chair
Were really still there:
God still saw them when you had gone out!

Dr. Johnson kicked stones and said, "Thus
I refute this ridiculous fuss!
They may think I'm dense,
But I've got Common Sense."
He was surely an ornery cuss.

Do you think we have learned any more
Than our ancestors knew back before?
Now the Chair and the Table
Are only a fable;
The Room has a lock on the door.

Deconstruction has buried the key
In the depths of the Post-Modern sea.
So we all stand around
Or we sit on the ground,
And we call it the freedom to *be*.

Piano (n.): One of the two instruments (cf. *Organ*) handed down by God to Adam and Eve in the Garden of Eden, on which all church music must be played.

Piety 1 (n., archaic): Reverence for God which affects the way one lives; 2 (n., current): Sanctimony.

Pilgrimage (n.): A visit to an important religious site, such as Wheaton or Colorado Springs.

Pin, Head of (n.): In Roman *Catholicism* (q.v.), the traditional venue where *Angels* (q.v.) hold their dances so that *Theologians* (q.v.) can try to count them. In Protestant *Fundamentalism* (q.v.), of course, the *Angels* do not dance.

Pious (adj.): Insufferable.

Plato (n.): Ancient *Philosopher* (q.v.) and disciple of *Socrates* (q.v.) who taught that houses and chairs were an allusion to Ideas we could never have because human beings really live chained in caves. This teaching gave rise to many ideas and trends in Christian *Theology* (q.v.), including its tendency to be pursued mainly by Troglodytes.

Poetry (n.): That one of the *Arts* (q.v.) which every major popular Christian periodical claims to support but refuses to publish.

Point 1 (n.): One of the three arbitrary sections into which the body of the *Sermon* (q.v.) is randomly divided by *Alliteration* (q.v.); so named from the gesture, involving the wagging or jabbing of the *Preacher's* (q.v.) index finger at the *Congregation* (q.v.), which often accompanies the *Alliteration*. 2 (n.): A marker of how Calvinistic one's *Theology* (qv.) is, ranging from zero to five. These *Points* correspond either to the number of Stars or of Rotten Tomatoes (depending on one's view) which the *Preacher* (q.v.) or *Theologian* (q.v.) is awarded. In a remarkable display either of self-aggrandizement or self-immolation (a great debate rages over which), one *Preacher* from Minneapolis claims to have seven.

Politics (n.): That which must not be discussed with one's in-laws; that to which previous generations of Evangelicals thought their theology irrelevant until the Baby Boomers substituted it for *Worship* (q.v.) and *Evangelism* (q.v.) as the primary expression of their Christian faith—causing *their* children to return to the error of their grandparents.

Politics, Church (n.): Loving cooperation in the *Administration* (q.v.) of the Lord's work, employing the time-honored methods of duplicity, subterfuge, and back-stabbing.

Pope, The (n.): The Bishop of Rome, head of the Roman Catholic Church; variously viewed as the Vicar of Christ or the Antichrist, depending on who is asking and who holds the office at the moment.

Potluck (n.): A communal meal in honor of the goddess Fortuna to which either everybody brings bean casserole or everybody brings dessert. The latter eventuality is much to be preferred, but cannot be counted on.

Postlude (n.): The attempt by the organist to drown out the criticism of the *Sermon* (q.v.) during the mass exit following the *Benediction* (q.v.).

Post-Modernism (n.): That period that comes between *Modernism* (q.v.) and Post-Post-Modernism. Modernists think that Science makes it possible for us to know everything perfectly and objectively, and that therefore all claims to know anything that can't be put into a test-tube or under a microscope are illusory; Post-Modernists think that Modernism was wrong, and that therefore we can't know anything at all. This is considered a great advance in human knowledge. Modernists think that anyone (except a Scientist) who makes a universal truth claim is a great fool; Post-Modernists think that anyone at all who makes a universal truth claim is a sly devil who is trying to gain power over you. Both are relativists, but while the Modernist is absolutely relative, the Post-Modernist is relatively more relative. The Post-Modernist also uses more jargon, like "metanarrative," "totalizing discourse," "sexual politics," and "hegemonic power structure," words which, when fully "deconstructed," all basically mean, "My, look how devilishly clever and up to date I am!"

Modernity's paternity
Produces Post-Modernity,
Where Power is the only good
That can by man be understood.
So Truth is just a sly digression
To serve the interests of Oppression

And anything that sounds sermonic
Just deconstructs to the ironic,
False oppressive rabbit trails
From Dead White European Males.
Extra syllables are the bargain
That we get by using jargon.
Extra meaning? Don't be square!
There wasn't ever any there.
Jargon! Would you like a sample?
Consider this one, for example:
We don't "write books" (the old construction);
Now we call it "text production,"
Where, doubling syllables, we add
The sly hint that the old is bad.
Words of beauty, verse that rhymes,
Are not suited to the times.
Rhythm and alliteration
Are a vile abomination.
Like the plague, all now do flee
Metaphor and Simile.
Detect an Author in the Text?
You'll want to find a Meaning next!
If any 'twixt the lines is tucked,
Poof! We make it deconstruct.
We abhor the putrid scent
Of old Authorial Intent.
In our hermeneutic blender,
Everything's reduced to Gender:
Illustrations of the sin
Of Dead White European Men.
If the work makes any sense,
It only proves the author's dense

And is a vain and snobbish prig.
For Meaning, then, give not a fig!
Only an archaizing fool
Would break this, our most basic rule.
No, let him not ask us to read
Aught with meanings there to heed.
Fractured prose, thoughts torn asunder
Fill the reader's heart with wonder,
And leave her with no grounds to tell
The path to Heaven from that to Hell;
And set us free to fill the nation
With any old Interpretation,
Immune from being proven wrong
Or right. And thus the Muses' song
Becomes (it's our firm resolution)
An instrument of prostitution
Designed to keep us (aren't we clever?)
In our tenured jobs forever!

Praise and Worship (n.): *Hymns* (q.v.) with half the words and half the chords left out. The remaining words are projected onto the wall and repeated infinitely to make up for the ones that are missing.

Pray (v., t.): To attempt to either (a) impress the congregation with one's piety, rhetorical skills, and mastery of Elizabethan English; (b) compete with the pastor by sneaking an extra sermon surreptitiously into the service; or (c, archaic and rare) converse with the Deity.

Prayer 1 (n.): The attempt to rationalize a course of action known to be underhanded, lowdown, mean, and back-stabbing, as in the sentence, "A lot of *Prayer* has gone into this decision." 2 (n., archaic and rare): Conversation with the Deity.

Prayer Request 1 (n.): *Gossip* (q.v.); 2 (n.): A way of seeking attention; cf. *Share.*

Preach (v., t.): To attempt, by means of a verbal harangue ostensibly based on a passage from the Bible, to render ineffectual the rational capacity of the congregation so that they will become and/or remain susceptible to the influence of the religious body sponsoring said oratory. Preachers differ in the means used to achieve this goal, the three most popular being sheer boredom, incredible sophistry, and emotional hype and manipulation.

Preacher (n.): One employed by the Church to keep its members entertained or asleep and everyone else driven away (see *Preach*). As famous Church Historian Ambrose Bierce notes, those preachers who make monkeys of themselves are known as harangue-outangs.

> There once was a prominent pastor
> Who was a proficient bombaster.
> He ranted so loud
> That the bulk of his crowd
> Had to come with their ears stuffed with plaster.

Preachy (adj.): Conveying a moral exhortation which makes one uncomfortable. Those utterances which make others uncomfortable are referred to as "relevant," "a word in season," "wise," or "incisive."

Predestination (n.): That which neither *Calvinists* (q.v.) nor *Arminians* (q.v.) understand, but both debate.

> All night long, we'd sat up and debated
> If Man is free, or if his will is fated
> To choose as it has been predestinated;

Or, if Man is responsible and free
By God's immutable and fixed decree,
Yet God rules all by strict necessity,
How can necessity and freedom mix?
The whole thing left my mind in such a fix
That I went walking, trying to explain
It all, and so got caught out in the rain.

The first drops turned to steam upon the road,
But soon they all came thick and fast, and flowed
Together. It was possible to tell
The precise moment they no longer fell
Directly on the pavement with a hiss,
But joined to form a watery abyss
That rushed to pile itself up in a heap
Along the curbs, and soon was ankle deep.

And all that water *had* to go downhill
Until it found some river it could fill,
Which, in its turn, would have to find the sea.
They did not ask advice from you or me,
Or stop to talk abstruse theology,
But just went on about their business, free
To be what their own natures bade them be.

Prelude (n.): The attempt by the organist to drown out the *Gossip* (q.v.) in the *Sanctuary (q.v.)* prior to the beginning of the *Service* (q.v.).

Premarital Counseling (n): The futile attempt to suggest that something more than active hormones and good intentions is required for a successful marriage. Said hormones will ensure that the counselees will agree with everything that is going in one of their ears and out the other.

Preparation (n.): That which Preachers and Sunday-School Teachers avoid until Saturday night.

> You cannot force the sovereign Muse
> To lend her aid to grace your views,
> For if you try, she will refuse.
> And your foul fate (it cannot miss)
> Will be to write a poem like *this!*

Preposition (n.): That with which one should not end a sentence. Winston Churchill considered this rule arrant pedantry, up with which he would not put.

Presbyterian (n.): One who believes that John Bar Zebedee and John Mark were actually pre-incarnate appearances of John Calvin and John Knox.

Presocratics (n.): Ancient Greeks who were trying to commit *Philosophy* (q.v.) before it was invented by Socrates. They appear to have spent a lot of time arguing about how many times one could cross a river, which proves that they were all wet.

> Men once thought that it would be nice
> To step in the same river twice.
>   But then Heraclitus
>   As if just to spite us
> Said, "No! Once will have to suffice."
>
> "The water is flowing away;
> The new that arrives does not stay.
>   Therefore, my conclusion:
>   All else is illusion.

There is Change; that is all we can say."

Parmenides answered, "Not so!
The stream doth eternally flow.
    What is permanent's real;
    So, whatever you feel,
There's no motion and no place to go."

He went on, "Heraclitus, you dunce,
Why attempt such ridiculous stunts?
    With no motion or change,
    You can't even arrange
To step in the first river once."

Is the world all in flux or immutable?
The answers both seemed irrefutable.
    But while they were debating,
    Some children went wading,
Once—twice—and it seemed somewhat suitable.

Pride (n.): The tendency of one's neighbor to overestimate his own ability and importance; his failure to appreciate yours.

Priest (n.): A *Preacher* (q.v.) in a clerical collar. They tend to use fewer and more predictable words with more stylized gestures.

Promotion (n.): The attempt by *Publishers* (q.v.) to actually sell books by informing the reading public that they exist. This is done only for those authors who already have so much name recognition that their books would sell like hotcakes without it.

Prooftext (n.): A passage of Scripture which can be made to support any position or course of action which seems attractive at the moment. Scripture was written to provide us with these useful sound bytes. They are obscured by *Context* (q.v.), so that they are revealed only to the faithful willing to persevere in obstinately looking hard for them.

Though his argument hardly was terse
And was bolstered by verse after verse,
The more that he quoted,
The audience noted,
The more his defense sounded worse.

Prophecy 1 (n., Pentecostal/Charismatic): Nonsense so vague that it is possible to blame it on the Deity. 2 (n., Dispensationalist): That which takes the place of Science Fiction in the *Christian Subculture* (q.v.).

Protectorate (n.): That period of history (the 1650's) in which Oliver Cromwell protected the nation of England from such evils as episcopacy, freedom of speech, and freedom of religion. Previously, the King had performed these useful functions, with the exception of protecting England from the evil of presbytery rather than episcopacy; at the end of this experiment, his son was invited back from vacation on the continent to resume his former role. Cf. *Interregnum*.

Protestant (n.): One who is not Roman *Catholic* (q.v.) and not Greek *Orthodox* (q.v.). Some have gone so far as to be not *Christian* (q.v.).

Publisher (n.): A commercial operation whose function is to put books into print and then not lift a finger to sell them. See *Promotion*.

Pulpit (n.): A piece of furniture, similar to a lectern or podium, but bigger and more pretentious to match the person standing behind it.

> Come and hear the bold expounder,
> Pastor Peter Pulpit Pounder,
> Rife with points opposing sin
> Punctuated by the din
> Of massive fists that beat them in.

Purgatory (n.): For Catholics, a place of temporal punishment and cleansing preparatory to Heaven; for Protestants, life.

Puritanism (n.): According to H. L. Mencken, "The haunting fear that someone, somewhere, may be happy." Like Fundamentalism, only more boring.

Q

Q (n.): Alleged source used by the biblical writers in the composition of the Gospels. But since we now know that the Greek manuscripts were translated from the original King James, this theory has no credibility.

Quarterly (n.): A periodical read to Sunday-School students in lieu of teaching them.

Quiet Time (n.): A daily period of Bible reading, meditation, and prayer, normally neglected either upon first rising for the day or just before retiring for the evening; cf. *Devotions*.

R

Rapture (n.): That which causes cars to be unmanned.

Reader Response Criticism (n.): The theory, promulgated by Stanley Fish, that a text means whatever the readers (or "interpretive community") want it to mean. Thought strangely to be an innovation, though, without knowing it, Christians have been practicing it for years.

> "I never," protested Stan Fish,
> "Said that readers can make what they wish
> Of a Text. The *community*
> Has that impunity."
> Slippery animals, fish.

Reason (n.): The set of perverted rules and principles by which *Intellectuals* (q.v.) and other deviants attempt to distinguish sense from nonsense, truth from error, etc.

Received Text (n.): See *Textus Receptus*.

Reconciliation 1 (n, archaic): The act of transforming enmity into friendship, as between God and man, or one man and another; 2 (n. current): unknown.

Recovery (n.): That stage of *Denial* (q.v.) in which one admits that one's problems exist but pretends to be solving them.

Redundant (adj.): Saying the same, exact, identical thing over and over and over and over again, too many times, excessively. A common characteristic, mark, quality, feature, and attribute of the homily, message, sacred lecture, Bible lesson, or *Sermon* (q.v.).

> Where words are too abundant
> They may become redundant,
> Leading us to say,
> "In our modern contemporary world of today,"
> Or causing us to write,
> "In the late, nocturnal night,"
> Or leading us to shout,
> "Chop, cut, and take them out!"

Refectory (n.): What monks call the *Fellowship Hall* (q.v.).

Reformation (n.): The movement in the Sixteenth Century when an impious group of rabble-rousers, heretics and malcontents tried to recall the Church to irrelevant and outmoded practices such as commitment to the apostolic Gospel; a process of renewal, refinement, and recommitment to its roots which the Protestant Reformers of the Sixteenth Century intended to be ongoing in the Church. Unfortunately, this intention, like all the best laid plans of mice and men, hath ganged aft agley.

Relevance (n.): That which causes a temporary spike in attendance, such as announcing a series of sensationalist sermons on the *End Times* (q.v.).

Repent (v., i.): To substitute one set of vices for another, as to replace smoking and drinking with gossip and judgmentalism.

Resolution (n.): A device which enables the delegates to denominational national conventions to assuage their consciences by voting to make pompous pronouncements on various social problems and issues which they have ignored the rest of the year.

Revelation (n.): That book of Scripture a series on which can always be counted on for a temporary spike in attendance.

Revival 1 (n., archaic): A religious awakening in which substantial numbers of Christians actually start to act like it, causing evangelism as a byproduct; 2 (n., current): A protracted series of meetings focused on evangelism, in the absence of the phenomenon referred to in the older definition and in the unflagging faith that effects can produce causes.

Righteousness 1 (n., archaic): The state of corresponding morally with the character of God, expressed in obedience to his commandments motivated by love; 2 (n., current): unknown.

Round John Virgin (n.): A short, portly servant who was present in the Stable at Bethlehem.

Rowling, J. K. (n.): A person who weighs the same as a duck; a recruiting agent for Wicca whose fiction has *nothing* to say about love or grace or anything else remotely related to or derived from the Christian faith.

J. K. Rowling
Was nothing if not controlling:
Foreordaining in her prep
Harry Potter's every step.

Voldemort:
Omitting his name made Harry snort.
He thought it silly and absurd
To be so fearful of the word.

Rubric (n.): Instructions marked in red in the Service Book; no doubt a reference to the fact that they contain coded clues to solving that labyrinthine ecclesiastical puzzle, the *Rubric's Cube.* See *Allegory.*

S

Sacrament (n.): What more formal churches call the *Ordinances* (q.v.; cf. *Baptism, Lord's Supper*). Christians disagree on whether the sacraments are seven, two, or zero in number, but they all agree that they are to be practiced for reasons which no one can remember.

Sacred Desk (n.): What the *Preacher* (q.v.) calls the *Pulpit* (q.v.) when he is indulging in *flowery* (q.v.) language.

Saint 1 (n., biblical): Any true believer in Christ; 2 (n., Roman Catholic); a spiritual superstar; 3 (n., popular): any personage from current times or church history of whom the speaker approves.

Salvation (n.): A fire insurance policy offered by the church to its *Members* (q.v.) in return for mindless agreement, tithes, and attendance.

Sanctification (n.): A species of *Denial* (q.v.) in which one is believed to have amassed, through responding to innumerable *Altar Calls* (q.v.), enough merit to mask one's remaining self righteousness and spiritual pride.

Sanctification, Entire (n.): That form of *Denial* (q.v.) taught by *John Wesley* (q.v.; cf. *Christian Perfection*); intended as an encouragement to righteousness; but since Christians appear to be incapable of distinguishing righteousness from self-righteousness, it has become an excellent source of spiritual *Pride* (q.v.).

Sanctuary (n.): Church-speak for *Auditorium*; no doubt a reference to the more sanctimonious individuals found in such venues.

Satan (n.): The true hero of both the Bible and *Paradise Lost*; his beneficent role in the liberation of humankind was suppressed by the Roman Catholic Church when it rewrote the Bible to eliminate all references to Jesus' marriage to *Mary Magdalene* (q.v.); cf. *Lucifer*.

Satire (n.): A literary genre in which wit, irony, and humor are used to make a serious critique of some practice or institution in society. Because there is clearly nothing in the Church of Jesus Christ that is worthy of such criticism, *Satire* obviously has no place in this Dictionary.

Saved 1 (adj): Having "gone forward" at an *Altar Call* (q.v.); 2 (n.): Those to whom the adjective applies.

Sawdust Trail (n.): The *Aisle* (q.v.) in a *Tent Meeting* (q.v.). Because the original Tabernacle in the Wilderness was a tent, because the Apostle Paul was a tentmaker, and because similar structures know as "Big Tops" house the Three-Ring Circus, that closest modern analog to the Church and its *Service* (q.v.), *Altar Calls* (q.v.) which take place using these *Aisles* are considered to be doubly efficacious.

Sawdust Trail, To Hit (v., t.): To respond to an *Altar Call* (q. v.) in a *Tent Meeting*. Only being saved in a Rescue Mission adds a greater cachet to one's *Testimony* (q. v.).

> If your sin's too much drinking of ale,
> If it be too much thinking at Yale;
> Whatever you've done,
> The atonement's begun
> At the end of the old Sawdust Trail.

If all of your virtue is frail
But all of your vices are hale,
        Get up out of your seat!
        Come down front; let us meet
At the end of the old Sawdust Trail.

If you're caught in the old Devil's spell
And your feet feel as slow as the snail,
        Just lift up your eyes!
        For Heaven's the prize
At the end of the old Sawdust Trail.

Sayers, Dorothy L. (n.): English wench who was not a member of the infamous *Inklings* (q.v.) but should have been. She corrupted true Christianity by writing about a drunk detective, by translating *Dante's* (q.v.) *Divine Comedy*, whose title suspiciously seems to imply that it is OK to have a sense of humor, and by maintaining that "The dogma is the drama," a remark which betrays its Satanic origin by encouraging people to attend the public theater.

Schaeffer, Francis: Popular Christian teacher of the 60's and 70's whose ideas and practices are still referred to and often praised but seldom understood or followed.

Scholarship 1 (n.): A financial award made to students, who need it because *Tuition* (q.v.) is so high; it is set so high so that the college can afford to offer *Scholarships*. 2 (n.): The attempt to elucidate a given text, idea, or topic by burying it under six feet of jargon; practiced by *Philosophers* and *Theologians* (q.v.).

When writing a long dissertation,
A man made a sound observation:

"Once I get the degree,
All this rubbish, with glee,
I will burn in a great conflagration!"

Scofield, C. I. (n.): The scholar employed by King James to write the original text of Scripture; cf. *King James Version*.

Scofield Notes (n.): The Fundamentalist answer to the infallibility of the Roman Catholic Teaching *Magisterium* (q.v.); cf. *Text*.

Screwtape (n.): Real author of a diabolical manual of temptation, ghost-written by C. S. Lewis, which contains no irony or humor whatsoever. The real Screwtape wishes it stated for the record that he stoutly maintains that (A) he does not exist; (B) the libelous material about his character inserted into his manual by C. S. Lewis was all malicious lies and slanders; (C) he has never lost a patient; (D) he does not know anybody named Wormwood; and (E) he had *absolutely nothing* to do with the composition of this Dictionary.

Scripture (n.): The source of *Prooftexts* (q.v.); the *Bible* (q.v.), considered as such.

Security, Eternal (n.): The doctrine that anyone who has ever "gone forward" at an *Altar Call* (q.v.) is saved forever and can never be lost again. Prying into irrelevant factors such as the person's grasp of the Gospel or commitment to living the Christian life is strictly inappropriate.

Seeker Sensitive (adj.): Pertaining to an evangelistic strategy in which one attempts to attract new members by pretending not to be a Church.

Seminary (n.): 1 (liberal/mainline): A place where future ministers are prepared to undermine the Church's integrity and belief structure lest it survive and prosper and fulfill its mission. 2 (conservative/ evangelical): A place where future ministers are trained to do things that every church needs but no church wants and few will tolerate.

Separation (n., archaic): The doctrine that Christians are supposed to be recognizably different from the *World* (q.v.) and to avoid compromising entanglements with it; that they are, in other words, to be in the *World* but not of it. 2 (n., current): The doctrine that since Christians are supposed to be different from the *World* (q.v.), they must therefore avoid both all contact with it and as much knowledge of it as possible.

Separation, of Church and State (n.): The provision in the Constitution by which the Founding Fathers thought they were prohibiting a state (or "*established*," q.v.) Church, since magically transformed by the Supreme Court into the principle that neither should meddle with the other at all and that the State's various organs (such as the public schools) should pretend that the Church does not exist or have any legitimate influence over or role in public life whatsoever. Variously appealed to by either side when it thinks it sees an advantage in doing so.

Separation, Secondary (n.): The doctrine that the only way Christians can maintain their purity is to avoid all contact not only with the *World* (q.v.) but also with most other Christians; also called *Second-Degree Separation*.

Septuagint (n.): That form of the Greek Old Testament into which the original King James was translated.

Sermon (n.): A species of oratory delivered by *Preachers* (q.v.). Highly effective as either an anesthetic or as a stimulant, depending on the character of both preacher and audience.

> When trying to wax sermonical
> With locutions both rich and thrasonical,
> Your rhetorical ploys
> Are nothing but noise
> If the content is dumb and moronical.

Sermon Notes 1 (n.): Slips of paper passed from one member of the *Congregation* (q.v.) to another during the *Sermon* (q.v.). 2 (n.): That which is ignored by the Preacher along with the *Watch* (q.v.) during the Sermon.

Sermonette (n.): A homily designed for the Christianette.

Sermonic (adj.): Soporific.

Service (n.): Church-speak for the rigmarole, hoopla, and folderol that takes place between the *Prelude* q.v.) and the *Postlude* (q.v.); what or whom precisely is "served" by these shenanigans remains something of a mystery.

Sex (n.): Hey, we can't talk about that here. This is a *Christian* Dictionary!

Share (v., t.): The use of *Prayer Requests* (q.v.) or *Testimonies* (q.v.) as excuses to indulge in exhibitionism and/or narcissism.

Sheep (n.): The *Goats* (q.v.) which belong to one's own fold (cf. *Denomination*).

Sheep Stealing (n.): *Evangelism* (q.v.) practiced by other denominations.

Sheol (n.): What theologians call *Hell* (q.v.); the place of eternal punishment reserved for pagans, infidels, intellectuals, and members of other *Denominations* (q.v.).

Silence (n.): The sound which follows the request for volunteers. In all other situations it is most assiduously to be avoided, as it might lead to the commission of some horrible sin such as *Thought* (q.v.).

> Wittgenstein
> Was known to opine,
> "Whereof we cannot speak,
> We ought to shut our beak!"

Sin 1 (n.): What one calls the imperfections, mistakes, and misbehavior of others. 2 (v., i.): For others to engage in such activities.

Sin, Unpardonable (n.): The act of questioning anything, especially the received opinions or edicts of the received *Tradition* (q.v.), authority, or clique on the ruling *Board* (q.v.); cf. *Philosophize, Thought*; cf. also *Sex*.

Sins, the Seven Deadly (n.): A medieval classification of the dispositions of the soul that lead to specific acts of evil (Pride, Envy, Wrath, Sloth, Avarice, Gluttony, and Lechery); too intelligent to be part of popular Evangelical lore, except as a reference to a movie. Since Fundamentalists do not watch movies, they have to practice the Seven without even knowing it.

> Behold Mankind, the noble creature,
> Like a god in every feature:

No sooner born than he begins
To seek the Seven Deadly Sins
(And others too, without a label,
He does as soon as he is able).
First comes PRIDE, the subtle foe
Which first begins this tale of woe.
Before the baby leaves his crib
Or even learns to wear a bib,
He makes his parents stoop and bow
And serve his every whim *right now*!
Bring the bottle or the breast,
Do not take our time for rest.
Rock him 'til he falls asleep
Or a vigil he will keep.
If ever they fall in arrears,
He'll avenge himself with tears.
He knows himself to be no worse
Than Center of the Universe,
Until his elders finally
Remember that they and not he
Are in control (for they are bigger).
This knowledge causes them to snigger,
And then a Schedule to enforce.
The baby yells until he's hoarse,
But only thus he learns to live
Somewhere between Take and Give.
ENVY next we have to mention,
For it is Pride's first invention
When it has to deal with things
That time inevitably brings.
When the family's escalated,
Things become more complicated:

Siblings come into his life
With new occasions for strife.
Whatever toy his sib desires,
To *that* one he himself aspires,
And that alone. No other one
Will do, could possibly be fun.
(That is, of course, until his brother
Decides himself to want another.)
'Til Envying what another hath
Inevitably leads to WRATH.
The toy not yielded, in despite,
There now proceeds a screaming fight,
That certain high-pitched, piercing whine
Which means, "You give that back—it's *mine*!"
A sound that every parent learns
To recognize. When Envy burns
It gives off flames of Wrath, and this
Also: the smoke of AVARICE.
Never let your children see
The toy commercials on TV.
The more it costs, the more they'll cry
That that's the one you *have* to buy
(Also the easier it breaks
And more assemblage that it takes)
'Cause *everybody* else has one,
And he alone never has any fun.
(Of course the toy box is already
Fuller than the wallet of J. Paul Ghetty
With good toys that they never use.)
So only let them watch the News!
Now, ever since old Adam's curse,
Things have gone from bad to worse.

Continue to observe this child,
Like a lamb so meek and mild:
During meals he seems a monk;
There is no place in all his trunk
For veggies or for casserole.
Starve the body, feed the soul!
Until the pious hermit sees
The Golden Arches through the trees.
French fries and potato chips
Slip so easily past his lips;
Candy, cakes, and pies withal
(As long as not one mineral
Or protein or a vitamin
Ever is allowed within).
Such is the sin of GLUTTONY
In a skinny tot of three.
Well, ever since old Adam's curse,
Things have gone from bad to worse.
Show me a Mom who has not said,
"Get in there and make your bed!
Pick you clothes up off the floor
So someone can get through the door!"
Now, he can run ten miles a day,
Lift weights, ride bikes, and swim, and play
At football. But go cut the grass?
You don't know what it is you ask!
To any such thing he is loathe:
He has learned the sin of SLOTH.
But e'er we reach the worst despair,
There shimmers in the chilling air
Perhaps the slightest sigh of hope:
"Maybe yet I still can cope.

So far, only six I see—
From *one* at least he will be free!"
Well, I don't like to see you frown,
But I will have to let you down:
Ever since old Adam's curse,
Things have gone from bad to worse.
His body is not made of wood;
He'd be LECHEROUS if he could!
Let him grow a few more years;
He will justify your fears,
And you will long for days of yore
With merely tantrums on the floor
To trouble your tranquility.
And if you ask, "How can this be?"
If you ask me, in a fit,
"Why then do we put up with it?"
My answer is a question too:
"Why does God put up with *you*?"

Slain in the Spirit (adj.): Suffering from a coma induced by a blow to the head. The lack of a subsequent diagnosis of concussion is clear proof of the Spirit's involvement.

Small Group (n.): A form of *Bible Study* (q.v.) designed to facilitate the pooling of ignorance.

Smart Phone (n.): A device for draining intelligence from the head next to which it is held.

Social Distance 1 (n): Six feet; a distance thought to be a protection from infection by COVID-19 because it is the distance that separates us from the dead after they are buried; 2 (vb, intrans.): To maintain a distance of six feet of separation from one's neighbor while he is still alive, in anticipation of the fact that "We are all going to die!"

Social Justice (n.): A scheme for addressing some social problem (usually more accurately described as "social mercy") that has been deliberately mislabeled in order to intimidate into silence, lest he be labeled "unjust," any opponent who might oppose it on purely prudential grounds.

Social Justice Warrior (n.): One who has confused *Karl Marx* (q.v.) with Jesus; an unwitting follower of those great peacemakers, ethicists, gentle examples, and social reformers Saint Vladimir of Lenin, Saint Joseph of Stalin, Saint Mao of Tse Tong, Saint Pol of Pot, Saint Che of Guevara, and Saint Kim of Jong Un.

Social Medium (n.): An oxymoron; a device for the amplification of antisocial behaviors such as *Gossip* (q.v.), *Virtue-Signaling* (q.v.), and theological *Disputation* (q.v.). When not engaging in these ministries, participants may indulge in actually edifying behaviors such as sharing pictures of one's breakfast or of one's cat.

Socrates (n.): Pagan geezer who was executed for the crimes of inventing *Philosophy* (q.v.) and asking a lot of stupid questions.

Socratic Method (n.): The attempt to teach by asking questions. Obviously inappropriate for use in Christian education, because we already know all the answers.

> When using the method Socratic,
> One shouldn't be *too* enigmatic:
> One cannot get blood
> From a turnip or spud,
> Or from stirring the dust in the attic.

Song Leader (n.): An officiant in Evangelical/Fundamentalist liturgy whose function is to omit verses from *Hymns* (q.v.) and wildly gesticulate at the congregation while they pretend to sing, exhorting them to greater enthusiasm. In this he usually fails, for the simple reason that enthusiasm must be present before it can be increased.

Soteriology (n.): That branch of *Theology* (q.v.) which is ignored in all discussions of salvation, the atonement, etc.

Spanish Inquisition (n.): That which nobody expects; the Roman Catholic approach to *Church Discipline* (q.v.); the examination, out of a pure sense of Christian Charity, of the beliefs of one's members, leading to a gentle remonstrance and patient instruction where required, using such enlightened educational methods as the Rack, the Stake, and the Iron Maiden.

Spargation (n.): A method of *Baptism* (q.v.); what *Theologians* (q.v.) call sprinkling (cf. *Effusion* and *Immersion*); so called because the water is used more sparingly than in the other methods.

Special (adj.): Just like everybody else (since, as we all know, "Everybody's *special*").

Special Music (n.): Two to three minutes of screeching introduced by ten minutes of rambling.

Specialty Bible (n.): An edition of Scripture with notes and apparati designed to appeal to a particular market niche, such as one-armed jugglers, left-handed former sanitation workers, or men recovering from having been divorced three times from the same woman.

Spurgeon, Charles (n.): Nineteenth century Preacher (q.v.) often taken as a role model today; primarily remembered for his beard and his cigars.

Spiritual 1 (adj., archaic): Godly; living a life *sub specie aeternitatis* which is characterized by such traits as love, joy, peace, longsuffering, gentleness, kindness, etc. 2 (adj., Baptist/Presbyterian/Independent): Boring. 3 (adj., Methodist/Episcopalian): Pagan. 4 (adj., Pentecostal/Charismatic): Able simultaneously to bark like a dog, babble like a goose, kick like a mule, lie like a rug, and laugh like an idiot.

Spirituality 1 (n., archaic): Godliness; cf. *spiritual*. 2 (n., current): The name of any one of the various strategies for avoiding contact with the Real World.

Stars through the Clouds: The Collected Poetry of Donald T. Williams, 2nd ed. Lantern Hollow Press, 2020. Futile attempt to restore poetic devices (meter, rhyme, form, etc.) to poetry and to restore poetry to favor with the reading public. Zealously to be avoided by *anyone* interested in Truth, Goodness, and Beauty.

Stewardship 1 (n., archaic): Considering one's time, abilities, and possessions as held in trust from God and hence managing them for His glory. 2 (n., current): *Tithing* (q.v.).

Study 1 (n., archaic): The deliberate, serious, and sustained application of the mind (for Christians, in dependence on the Holy Spirit and in submission to the Scriptures) to any problem for the purpose of attaining knowledge, understanding, and wisdom; a necessary part of spiritual discipline. 2 (n., current): A sometimes (for students) necessary evil to be avoided as much as possible, like death and taxes; the seedbed of pride.

There once was a student of lore
Who would study and study for more
    Than a day at a time.
    He went out of his mind,
And collapsed on the library floor.

There once was a student of grammar
Who was an incurable crammar.
    He studied his best
    On the eve of the test
By beating it in with a hammar.

Study Bible (n.): An oxymoron (as the two words are used by most contemporary Christians). See *Bible Study*.

Suffering for the Lord (n.): Incurring some serious inconvenience as a result of one's religious commitments, such as getting out of bed on Sunday morning.

Sunday School 1 (n.): An oxymoron. 2 (adj.): Shallow; insipid; boring.

Summer (n.): That period of the year in which attendance drops because the *Congregation* (q.v.) is traveling and taking their vacations. They usually do this while school is out, during the months of June, July, and August; therefore the drop in attendance typically lasts from mid April through mid October.

Supremacy, Act of (n.): The decision by Parliament in 1534 that it was better to have the King usurp the title of "Supreme Head of the Church in England" than to continue letting the Pope do so. Certain unreasonable people like Thomas More lost their heads and refused to subscribe to the oath attached to this entirely expedient proposal.

Survey 1 (v., t.): To ask questions about one's religious views and/or affiliation as an excuse for proselytizing. 2 (n.): A questionnaire, administered by Pollsters, on which all contemporary theology and church practice are based.

Sweet Singer of Israel, The (n.): A reference to the fact that David was saved out of a decadent and morally degrading career as a folk musician; but after repenting and cleaning up his life, he went into the much more honorable field of politics.

Swift, Jonathan (n.): Eighteenth-century Anglican priest who edited the diaries of Lemuel Gulliver, and whose essays such as "A Modest Proposal" and "An Argument against the Abolishing of Christianity in England" had no influence whatsoever on *The Devil's Dictionary of the Christian Church*.

> Jonathan Swift,
> When sufficiently miffed
> With the whole human race,
> Could put it in its place.

T

Tares among the Wheat (n.): One's neighbor, when sitting next to one in Church.

Telephone (n.): An instrument connecting a fool to a knave. One of the Church's greatest engineering triumphs, able to disseminate *Gossip* (q.v.) faster than a speeding bullet. Now superceded by the *Smart Phone* (q.v.) and *Social Media* (q.v.).

Temptation (n.): According to H. L. Mencken, "the operation of an irresistible force upon a movable body." According to Mark Twain in "The Man who Corrupted Hadleyburg," a necessary precondition of virtue. The impulse, often blamed upon the Devil but really only encouraged by him, to act according to Nature.

Tent Meeting (n.): A *Revival* (q.v., "current") held in a Tent, considered an appropriate location because of its resemblance to the traditional venue of a Three-Ring Circus.

Testimony (n.): Rambling and incoherent self-reportage of one's alleged spiritual progress; rambling and incoherent reportage of nobody knows what.

Tetzel, Johan (n.): Late Medieval Evangelist and Hawker of *Indulgences* (q.v.) whose stock tanked as a result of the *Reformation* (q.v.); inventor, in his more successful period, of the advertising jingle.

When the coin into the coffer rings,
The soul from Purgatory springs;
When the coin clinks in the chest,
The soul flies up to eternal rest.
— *Traditional*

Text 1 (n.): That part of Scripture which supplements the *Scofield Notes* (q.v.); 2 (n.): That portion of Scripture which is used as the pretext for the *Sermon* (q.v.).

The Preacher was always enlargin'
On Points where no Angel would barge in.
    The whole inspiration
    For these bold orations
Was Notes that he found in the Margin!

Textus Receptus (n., Lat.): That form of the Greek New Testament into which more scribes translated the original *King James* (q.v.) than any other.

Theater, Public (n.): That which *Fundamentalists* (q.v.) are forbidden to attend, lest they realize how much more entertaining it is than their *Services* (q.v.).

Theocracy (n.): That form of civil government in which the dominant *Denomination* (q.v.) makes everybody miserable on behalf of the Deity as punishment for their *Sins* (q.v.).

Theologian (n.): One who practices *Theology* (q.v.); one who wishes to edify the Church by addressing to fellow academics sentences which even they cannot understand.

When writing a long dissertation
On the doctrine of predestination,
    The Theologue froze,
    For the words that he chose
Were predestined to cause hibernation.

Theology 1 (n., archaic): The systematic exposition of the content of the Christian faith and its implications; "the science of living happily forever"; 2 (n., current): Obfuscation; the attempt to render the faith incomprehensible and irrelevant; a purely academic exercise in futility which true friends of the Church hope will continue to have no impact on her whatsoever.

Thermostat (n.): A device, ostensibly for regulating the temperature in the *Sanctuary* (q.v.), but which is incapable of any setting at which no member will complain; a device for guaranteeing that 50% of the *Congregation* (q.v.) will be sweltering while the other 50% freeze.

What is the worst theological spat
In ecclesiological tit for tat?
    Could it be inspiration
    Or predestination?
No, worse: adjusting the thermostat.

Thought 1 (n., archaic): The activity of the mind; it can be good or evil depending upon its object and whether it is done in dependence on the Holy Spirit and in submission to Scripture; a necessary prerequisite to and component of *Faith* (q.v.). 2 (n., current): A snare of the Devil, always a precursor of evil; incompatible with *Faith* (q.v.).

Tintinnabulation (n.): The sound, allegedly musical, produced by the Bell Choir.

Tithe 1 (v., t.): To give money to the Church in lieu of any other form of support, such as time or faithfulness. In traditional and archaic use, a specific figure of 10% of income was understood to be involved; current usage averages about 3–4% or less. 2 (n.): The pittance given.

Tolkien, J. R. R. (n.): Evil member of the *Inklings* (q.v.), promoter of the occult, and inventor of "Dungeons and Dragons." It is obvious that his books are totally perverse and Of The Devil and should never be read by Christians, because all of the Good Guys in them both smoke and drink.

Tongues, Speaking in (n.): *Glossolalia* (q.v.): A species of incoherent babbling considered highly edifying in some circles; in other words, like the *Sermon* (q.v.), but more honest, i.e., without the illusion of lucidity.

Total Depravity (n.): Human nature; *especially,* redeemed human nature.

Tract (n.): A small booklet conveying an evangelistic message, given to unsuspecting victims in lieu of witnessing to them, or to waitresses in lieu of a tip. *John Henry Newman* (q.v.) wrote some for The Times, but *The Times*, being a secular publication, declined to publish them.

Tradition 1 (n., archaic): Wisdom, in the form of words or practices, handed down to the Church by members of previous generations; not (for Protestants) authoritative like Scripture, but useful to avoid reinventing the wheel. 2 (n., current): "We've always done it that way," the ultimate justification for any ecclesiastical decision; proceeding from a slavish attachment to (and leading to rebellion against) what Ezra Pound called "the obvious imbecilities of one's immediate ancestors."

New ideas arouse great suspicion
Lest they clash with unwritten Tradition.
    "It's the way we have done it
    Since Time was begun; it
Just needs, then, your humble submission."

Transition (n.): A rhetorical device used in the *Sermon* (q.v.) to separate the foolishness from the nonsense; the nonsense from the balderdash; the balderdash from the horse feathers; and the horse feathers from the fish fuzz.

Tribulation (n.): A period of seven years in which really bad things happen to people who did not read the *Left Behind* series. The *Rapture* (q.v.) will occur either before, during, or after this period, depending on which constituency the *Theologian* (q.v.) is trying to impress. Cf. *Eschatology, End Times.*

Trite (ad.): The quality of a word, phrase, or idea's having been overused, abused, and run into the ground to the point that it becomes eligible for inclusion in a Sermon (q.v.) or religious poem.

When writing a verse that is light,
One should always avoid being trite.
    When you dish out advice,
    If you take it, that's nice.
Have I always done so? Not quite.

Truth 1 (n., archaic): That version of things which corresponds to the way they actually are, i.e., to the way God sees them; impossible for human beings to achieve in an absolute sense, but capable of being approximated through *Study* (q.v.), submission to Scripture and to evidence, and the application of tests, checks, and balances; the "sovereign good of human nature," and the duty of every person to pursue and, finding, to accept and live by. 2 (n., current): "The majority opinion of that nation which can lick all the other nations" (Oliver Wendell Holmes); that version of things which seems, at the moment, to be consistent with one's preconceived notions and to advance one's agendas. Since this is the best human beings can hope for, we might as well exploit the situation.

Tuition (n.): That which students are charged to attend the *Christian College* (q.v.) or *University* (q.v.); that which increases at twice the rate of inflation, while the faculty salaries increase at one half the rate of inflation, thereby calling into question the Law of the Conservation of Matter.

In pursuit of refined erudition,
We shell out big bucks for tuition.
    But where it all goes,
    There is no one who knows;
Though the Faculty have their suspicions.

Tulip (n.): Flower favored by *Calvinists* (q.v.) because it is grown in Holland, which, being the *Low* Country, reminds them of that place to which the great majority of mankind are predestined.

Tweet 1 (n.): A *Sermon* (q.v.), rant, or diatribe adapted to the attention span of a modern audience: approximately 1.5 seconds. 2 (vb., t.): To unleash such a helpful discourse upon the world, for the enlightenment and edification of mankind.

Twitter (n.): The original name (now "X") of a social medium even more efficiently adapted to the modern reader and the Spirit of the Age than *Facebook* (q.v.); the medium the Founding Fathers would no doubt have created for the reasoned political discourse on which the American Experiment in Representative Government depends had they foreseen what citizens would be like in the Twenty-First Century.

Typology (n.): That approach to *Hermeneutics* (q.v.) which holds that everything in Scripture is actually something else in Scripture, none of which has any bearing on anything outside of Scripture. This is known as the "hermeneutical circle."

U

University (n.): A place where young people are sent to lose their faith. If it survives anyway, sending them to *Seminary* (q.v.) will usually do the trick. (cf. *College*).

Unspoken Prayer Request (n.): An invitation to speculation.

Usher (n.): One of an army of functionaries whose job is to find seats for *Late-Comers* (q.v.), take up the *Collection* (q.v.), and gossip in the back of the *Sanctuary* (q.v.).

V

Valla, Lorenzo (n.): Renaissance scholar who exposed the *Donation of Constantine* (q.v.) as a forgery, whereupon the Papacy meekly admitted its erroneous pretensions to temporal power and moved out of the Vatican.

Value (n.): That which the Religious Right wishes to impose on others. This is obviously a bad thing, because previous attempts to do so ended such profitable social practices as slavery, child labor, horrible prison conditions, etc.

Vatican (n.): The corporate headquarters of the multinational corporation known as the Roman Catholic Church. See *Catholic, Pope.*

Vatican II (n.): Twentieth-century church council which dumbed down the Mass by putting it into the common tongue of the base, vulgar herd of the unwashed multitude, or *Member* (q.v.), so that the *Liturgy* (q.v.) could be misunderstood by the *Laity* (q.v.) as well as the *Clergy* (q.v.). This set a bad example for *Protestants* (q.v.), who proceeded to dumb down their own services from English into Newspeak.

Vengeance (n.): An extra verse of "Just as I Am" added to the *Altar Call* (q.v.) as a response to the absence of any response.

Virtue (n.): What one calls the vices of others when they appear in oneself.

Wisdom, Justice, Fortitude
Make one rather seem a prude;
All things done in Moderation
Sends one into hibernation;
Faith and Hope and Charity
Are certainly a rarity.
Were it not that it can hurt you,
Vice would feel much more like virtue,
And too much zeal can sure suffice
To make a virtue seem a vice.
Since goodness then is but a rumor,
Best we keep our sense of humor.

Virtue-Signaling (n.): Letting one's light so shine before men that they may see one's good works and glorify ... wait, how does that verse end?

Vulgate (n.): What Roman Catholics claim to be the original text of Scripture. But since it has been shown that the Greek and Hebrew had already been translated from the original *King James* (q.v.) before the Latin Vulgate was written, this claim has no validity. Also, the Vulgate's obvious affinity to the *Textus Receptus* (q.v.) is very suspicious, since that version has already been defined as that form of the Greek Bible into which more scribes translated the original *King James* than any other. Ergo, Q.E.D.

W

Walk Through the Bible (n.): A form of theological Trivial Pursuit

Walton, Izaak (n.): Seventeenth-century fisherman and lover of good company, good poetry, and primitive Christianity, whose lives of John Donne and George Herbert provide accurate portraits of that hopelessly outdated form of Christianity designated as "archaic" in the definitions of this Dictionary, and whose *Complete Angler*, with its love of innocent mirth, had no influence whatsoever on the writer of this Dictionary.

Watch (n.): That device which the *Preacher* (q.v.) lays upon the *Pulpit* (q.v.) at the beginning of the *Sermon* (q.v.) and does not notice again until he collects his notes after the *Altar Call* (q.v.).

Weaker Brother (n.): He whom it is inconceivable to offend, no matter how strong, stubborn, and unreasonable his sensibilities or picayune his prejudices. Fortunately, Christians are compensated for this orgy of sensitivity by being given *carte blanche* to offend pagans, infidels, minorities, women, and intellectuals with gay abandon. After all, everybody knows that intellectuals do not really have any feelings, and the passage says nothing about weaker *sisters*, now, does it?

Wedding (n.): The necessary prelude to *Divorce* (q.v.).

Wedding Planner (n.): One whose job it is to make sure that newly married couples start life in a state of extreme poverty so that they are not tempted by Mammon.

Wesley, John (n.): Multi-talented church leader and founder of Methodism (see *Methodist*) who could simultaneously preach a sermon, write a book, and start a controversy while riding horseback.

Whitefield, George (n.): Eighteenth-Century Evangelist who could make thousands of people weep just by pronouncing the word "Mesopotamia." Many similar examples of bad enunciation exist today, but, being a more tolerant generation, we generally forbear to weep.

Wilberforce, William (n.): Eighteenth Century politician who perniciously mixed church and state with disastrous results for the slave trade, setting a bad precedent for other meddlers, such as the Religious Right and the Pro-Life movement, who wish to impose their personal beliefs and values on innocent secularists today.

Williams, Donald T. (n.): Archaic wannabe and therefore deservedly obscure poet and theologian who has absolutely no sense of humor whatsoever and did not write this Dictionary.

Wimpy, Okra (n.): The most popular and influential theologian at the beginning of the Twenty-first Century.

Wisdom 1 (n., archaic): The ability to use one's intelligence, knowledge, and understanding in ways that glorify God, advance His Kingdom, and benefit one's fellow man. 2 (n. current): That type of folly espoused by oneself or the group with which one identifies; the folly which seems most consistent with one's preconceived notions.

Witch Hunt (n.): The *Fundamentalist* (q.v.) approach to literary study; the benevolent attempt to rid the world, for its own good, of anything that weighs the same as a duck, such as spinsters in Salem, Mass., Harry Potter, or Narnia.

It seems that some shy intellectual Brit
(Most likely a Snob and most surely a Twit)
    Gets hit
    By a fit
    Of maniacal wit
That causes his neurons to splutter and split.
Well, once this gets started he just cannot quit
    'Til out he does spit
A Story that has at least one Naughty Bit.
    And when this mad fit
    Has finally flit,
    He finds he has writ,
    And that's how we get
The very great bulk of our classical Lit.,
Which exists so the Critics can critic their crit
    And so Christians can grit
    Their teeth as they sit
In bold and peremptory judgment on it
    And condemn every whit,
Seeing no reason why they should admit
    That so to conclude
    Without reading a word
    Would be horribly rude
    Not to mention absurd,
For they already know that it came from the Pit!

Witness 1 (v., i., archaic): To share one's experience of God's grace in Christ with sufficient biblical and theological context so that it can encourage faith on the part of the hearer; 2 (v., i., current): To engage (depending on one's denominational background and inclinations) either in hostile arguments over fine points of *Theology* (q.v.), or in unorganized gushing about nobody knows what; 3 (n.): The particular instance or content or perpetrator of any of the above.

Witnessing (n.): Subjecting one's victim to involuntary group therapy.

Workshop, the Devil's (n.): Idle hands, i.e., those engaged in the *Arts* (q.v.).

World, the 1 (n., archaic): The way of life naturally produced by the Fall. Christians are called to be in it but not of it. 2 (n., current): That which lies beyond the pale of the *Christian Subculture* (q.v.); that which Christians are called to reach but must never touch, for the slightest contact defiles both soul and body.

Worldly (adj.): Having convictions that differ from the speaker's.

Worship 1 (n., archaic): The active and intelligent ascription of worth to the Deity; the ordered expression, and by that expression the reinforcement, of the attitude toward and response to God appropriate to those redeemed by Him. 2 (n., current): A non-chemical drug, administered through emotional manipulation. *Denominations* (q.v.) differ on whether the pill should be an Upper or a Downer.

Worship Leader (n.): Mood Engineer; what the *Song Leader* (q.v.) is called in contemporary-style worship.

Worship Team (n.): Rock combo.

Worship Wars (n.): The struggle to impose on the entire church the style of music which one's own generation prefers; highly preferred to such vices as tolerance or forbearance, or to the danger of expanding one's range of taste or being exposed in one's worship to something horribly blasphemous, like an idea.

WWJD (n., acrostic): That theory of Christian ethics which holds that the proper solution to any problem is to wear a piece of jewelry asking, "What Would Jesus Do?" Unfortunately, no method of rationally ascertaining an answer to this question has yet been proposed.

X

Xanthippe (n.): A pagan wench, the wife of Socrates, who has absolutely no excuse for being in this Dictionary whatsoever, other than the fact that the author can spell her name and that she is able to supply another entry under X.

> Xanthippe
> Could be somewhat snippy.
> Her husband, Socrates, knew
> Her as rather a shrew.

Xmas (n.): A pagan holiday which is the centerpiece of a vast conspiracy to take Christ out of *Christmas* (q.v.). The argument that it is actually an abbreviation that comes from the fact that X, chi, is the first letter of "Christ" in the Greek alphabet is obviously fallacious, since the Greek is only a translation from the original *King James* and therefore has no authority.

Y

Young Christian's Survival Guide, The. Cambridge, OH: Christian Publishing House, 2019 (n.): Pestiferous book by that archaic wannabe *Donald T. Williams* (q.v.) which purports to provide answers to hostile questions frequently asked of Christians today. This book should *not* be read by *anyone* interested in understanding the grounds of the Christian faith or learning how to defend it.

Youth Group (n.): A device for segregating the adolescents in the *Congregation* (q.v.) lest they learn to participate in the life of the church. Cf. *Children's Church*.

Youth Pastor (n.): A functionary who is valued so highly, and whose appearance of commitment to his charges is known to be so critical to his success, that he is paid a salary which guarantees that he will be replaced annually.

Youth Retreat (n.): The opposite of a youth attack. The youth are often sent off on such a maneuver as a preemptive strike to prevent their attacking, lest they disturb the slumber of their parents during the *Sermon* (q.v.).

Z

Zeal (n.): Christian-speak for *motivation* (not to be confused with *habit*); that which causes people to show up for the *Service* (q.v.); that which, in sufficient amounts, might even cause people to *Tithe* (q,v,)

Zealot (n.): One who has more *Zeal* (q.v.) than the speaker approves, i.e., more than he has himself.

Zebra (n.): A striped animal who was on the Ark and who gives us the opportunity to have at least one entry under Z. Zebras are either black with white stripes or white with black stripes, proving that animals have *Denominations* (q.v.) too.

What's that on the zebra's back,
Black on white or white on black?
Conundrum to befuddle sight:
White on black or black on white?
Was the contrast then so stark
When Noah shooed them on the Ark?
Had they still such perplexing skin
When he let them off again?
Did Shem and Japheth hold debate
When the stormy nights got late
Over what the proper term is
For their divided epidermis?
Since we still cannot decide
How best to analyze their hide,

Let us leave them to the scholars
Who wear the black/white, backwards collars!

Zoo (n.): Church; any given congregation—take your pick.

Zwingli, Huldrych (n.): Protestant Reformer who is mainly remembered for coming at the end of theological dictionaries and for all the things he did not say about the *Eucharist* (q.v.).

APPENDIX A: A VIEW FROM BEYOND

Donald T. Williams, PhD, Translator

I have no intention of revealing how the following manuscript fell into my hands. The anonymity of my sources must not be compromised. I can say that it represents an attempt by an extraterrestrial anthropologist to study the religions of earth. Not being able to master the illogical grammar of human languages, he endeavored to reconstruct the contents of our sacred texts by studying the actual behavior of their adherents—surely a reasonable procedure, since they claim to base their lives on the teachings of those books. Here we present some excerpts from the version of the Bible which resulted from his observations of professing Christians.

Fortunately, he landed in the American Bible Belt among good, conservative, Bible-believing Evangelicals. No telling what kind of picture he would have gotten from the liberals! Since I have had some training in linguistics and had also picked up the rudiments of Old Solar by reading C. S. Lewis's Space Trilogy, I was asked to translate his thesis into English. But something seems to have gone wrong with his translation of the Bible. Maybe I've mistranslated—or can you think of some place where he might have gotten such ideas? For his Bible sounds—well, judge for yourself.

"Rejoice in the Lord sometimes, and again I say rejoice! Do not forsake the assembling of yourselves together unless the alarm doesn't go off, the fish are biting, or 'things are just a little hectic right now.' Let your no be no and your yes be maybe.

"Be not conformed to this world, but to the one of thirty years ago instead. Bodily exercise profiteth the health club. Though I speak with the tongues of men and angels and have not a recording contract, it profiteth me nothing. Let the redeemed of the Lord say so, but only in church in front of other Christians, and then only in safe, stereotyped testimonies, lest any be offended.

"A positive self image is the beginning of wisdom. If any man wishes to come after me, let him be healthy, wealthy, and wise. Whoever wishes to be great among you, let him use direct mail fund-raising. For what doth it profit a man to gain the whole world and lose his tax benefits? No one can serve two masters, but you can certainly try.

"If your brother hath aught against you, change churches. And the Lord gave some as apostles, some as prophets, and some as pastors and teachers, that the saints might pay their salaries and sit back to watch them do the work of the church. Study to present yourselves as workmen that need not to be ashamed, rightly dividing your investment opportunities. Let not many of you become teachers, my brethren, for such will have to spend time in preparation. Therefore, leaving the elementary teachings about Christ, let us press on to obscurity. Desire the sincere milk of the Word, and leave the meat to the theologians.

"Now, faith is the assurance of things wished for, the evidence of things not seen. For by it the men of old gained health and wealth. They were interviewed on talk shows, they were elected to boards, they published ghost-written autobiographies, men of whom the world was not worthy. If any among you lack wisdom, let him read self-help books and take assertiveness (or sensitivity) training. For this is pure and undefiled religion in the sight of Man: to have conferences about the widows and orphans in their distress and maintain a public image unspotted by the world.

"Anyone who divorces his wife, except for incompatibility, and marries another, commits adultery. Husbands, boss your wives as Christ—oh, never mind. Wives, be in submission to the National Organization for Women, and as far as your oppressive, male-chauvinist husbands are concerned, stand fast in the liberty with which Christ has set us free. For by psychology are ye saved through a positive self image, and that not of yourselves; it is the gift of Televangelists, that every man should boast."

Well, I have not had the heart to translate any further. But if it is true that Christians are the only Bible that some will ever read, I must tell you that this is all too often what the world is hearing. It gives a new meaning to a verse actually found in the real Bible:

"Jesus wept."

APPENDIX B: THE CHRISTIAN SCHOLAR AS DECONSTRUCTIONIST

To approach the task of Christian Education from a neo-presuppositional, Evangelical point of view, we must first understand the relevance of Florentine neoplatonic hermeneutics to pre-grammatical allegorical eisegesis. This, of course, is based on an analysis of the latent psychological tendencies of the post-adolescent Homo Loquens, with her utter lack of critical and intellective faculties, or, as it is known to the base, vulgar tongue of the common multitude, the principle of *Canis in corpore transmuto*.

Of course, when the *Ding an Sich* is ingested by the Hegelian world spirit, a dynamic afflatus is engendered, in inverse ratio to the presence or absence of a vegetative soul in asymmetrical relationship to the square root of pi, with the inevitable result that there is a most grievous and prodigious exhalation, release, and ejection of a diffused and distended substance not unlike, and bearing an analogous relationship to, gas, or, with due respect to the canons of Renaissance self fashioning, wind.

While such epistemological considerations can have the lamentable effect of inducing a state of angst, nausea, and psychological deviance on the part of the proctor, the ability to step in the same river twice, acquired by a diligent application of stoic inertia, should allow the student simultaneously to achieve stasis and to evolve toward the omega point of unity with the unfolding dialectic of his own navel. All charges of solipsism should be assiduously ignored on the grounds that we exist, therefore we are. When the involutions of the convoluted aspects of bovine meditation are properly integrated with the assured results of modern criticism, the accretion of jargon is assured. Notwithstanding, we should beware of the temptation to reify actuality in terms of the categories of Non-Being, apart from which there is no recourse to anything less than an admission that whereof we cannot speak, we must be silent.

Silence is then the final word uttered by the cacophany of fresh-person writing, couched in the allusion to an illusion of intelligible peroration. Therefore, I exhort you: eschew, by pursuing, the *tabula rasa*, on which there is neither subject nor object, surface nor depth, impression nor obduracy, but only the cosmic blankness of the pre-rational psyche. Let us inscribe thereon rather in contradistinction the contrapuntal effluvia of the Isidorian Decretals lest, caught in a backfire from the Canons of Dordt, we find our post-modern detachment dissolving in deconstruction, leaving us no alternative but to make, in spite of our best and brightest efforts to the contrary, some sense.

To conclude in brief and plain English: *Ad hominem, ex post facto cum corpus dilecti, quod inductio ex absurdum; argal, Q.E.D.*

(The question of the propriety, ethicality, and or admissibility of professorial exploitation of the captive audience syndrome for pecuniary gain is a fascinating one which need not detain us here. Suffice it to say that it was addressed in the case of State of California vs. S. I. Hiawatha, 1983, with predictable results. *Argal, Q. E. D.)*

Onalday Illiamsway, PhD

APPENDIX C: THE BAPTISTRY CODE

Note: Any resemblance to a popular novel by Dan Brown is purely coincidental.

Plankton stared glumly at the back wall of the little baptist church in rural America. The Yale symbologist shook his head. There it was again, another version of the same mural he kept seeing painted behind every baptistry, the tank above the choir loft where these strange Christians practiced their stranger ritual of ceremonial dunking. It was there too often to be a coincidence: a picture of the River Jordan—flowing through the English countryside! He knew the artists were trying to tell him something. The connectivity was there, just below the surface, if only he could dive down to the bottom of it.

And then it hit him. That fool from Harvard had it all wrong! The whole Palestine thing was a ruse created by Joseph of Arimathea to hide the truth: Jesus had never set foot in the so-called Holy Land at all. He was a Celtic river god worshipped in England when it was known as Roman Britain. No Palestinian peasant from the First Century could possibly have had that kind of power. It all fit: the importance of ablution, the ceremonial meal, obviously a thinly disguised version of the Cauldron of Plenty. The Roman Catholic Church and their Protestant dupes had been carefully guarding this secret for 2,000 years, but now it was uncovered at last!

But wait. Would anybody believe him now that *The DaVinci Code* was already a best seller? How diabolically brilliant of Rome to create this diversion just in time to discredit his discovery! Langdon was being used, that much was certain. But by whom? Let's see now, think! Think! DaVinci Code, the movie—directed by Ron Howard, whose secret true identity was ... Opie? Hmmm, Opie, Opie ... OPUS! *Opus Dei*! That was it.

It was all clear now, all too clear. His discovery was useless. With *Opus Dei* having already cornered the market—how clever of them to pretend to be discrediting themselves!—people would only think Plankton's Baptistry Code was, er, all wet. He decided to drown his sorrows. It was the only thing left to do.

B. S. Clueless
AKA Donald T. Williams, PhD

APPENDIX D: 101 THINGS TO DO WITH A DEAD CHURCH

By Mark A. Gerl

PREFACE

Unfortunately, dead churches are becoming more and more commonplace in 21st century America. People still attend, programs continue, and yet all of the true life is gone. The members are bereft of the joy of being Christians. They hold to their programs and dogma so seriously, that they choke out the life of freedom to which we were born again. They are, for all intents and purposes, zombies. They move and function, but are far from alive.

While a traditional zombie can make for cheap labor (provided you can find a competent voodoo doctor and a fresh corpse), the only thing that ecclesiastical zombies are good for is to have some fun at their expense and hope to get thrown out (getting thrown out is preferred to merely leaving because that way you are almost always guaranteed to be taken off of the mailing list).

With this in mind, the following list was compiled to poke fun, make mischief, and wreak havoc in and to a dead church. After which, you are free to join a church that can appreciate a good joke.

101 THINGS TO DO WITH A DEAD CHURCH

1. Paint a submarine periscope in the Jordan River behind the baptismal.
2. Replace the chorus overhead with the words to Dirty Deeds Done Dirt Cheap by AC/DC.
3. Spike the communion juice.
4. Take a batch of Ex-Lax Brownies to the dessert social.
5. Lock the bathroom doors at the above-mentioned dessert social.
6. Try starting "the wave" instead of saying "Amen."
7. Replace wax candles with Roman candles for the candle-light service.
8. Deposit whoopee cushions in the choir loft.
9. Slip a copy of *Mein Kampf* onto the pastor's desk just before the District Superintendent stops in to say hello.
10. When you are served the communion bread, ask the usher, "Do you have any Grey Poupon?"
11. Regardless of the topic, after the service, ask the pastor, "Was the second point of your sermon in favor of goat sacrifice or just drinking ox blood?" (Bonus points are awarded for doing this in front of the DS).
12. Show up at a committee meeting in stretch pants and a bow tie, explaining that you are moonlighting as a Chippendale dancer (or Playboy bunny for female readers).

13. During Missions emphasis week, slip Cardassia in to the list of unreached people groups. (Author's note: if there are fewer than five Star Trek fans in the church, don't bother. The humor would be lost. Then again, if there are as many as five Star Trek fans, it probably isn't dead.)

14. Have copies of explosive material catalogs sent to the church address under one of the deacons' names.

15. Place flash pots on the stage and wait for a "Hellfire and Damnation" sermon. (However, be warned that if this stunt results in record numbers of Altar Call responses, you may be asked to repeat it over and over).

16. Volunteer to teach the Junior High boys Sunday School class about the Holy Spirit, or the tongues of fire at Pentecost, or just fire.

17. Post flyers for the church open house in the local biker bar.

18. When the church receives new members, rather than the traditional hug, greet them with a full dip kiss.

19. Pay your monthly tithe in pennies.

20. Pledge $1,000 a month to the building drive in some body else's name (preferably an elder or deacon).

21. When asked to introduce yourself in a Small Group setting, say, "I am Falkor, Dark Lord of the Universe; obey me, pathetic Earthlings!" using the classic "Darth Vader" voice.

22. Take the church bus to a hot rod shop. "Ten wheels, fifteen kids, zero to sixty in seven seconds flat!"

23. Take the youth group on a trip to Las Vegas. Ask for a couple hundred bucks for "entertainment expenses."

24. Propose a support group for Born Again Nazi Transvestites who have been abducted by aliens. Meet any resistance to the idea with the words "I feel led that there is a real need for this ministry."

25–30 SPECIAL SECTION:

"Fun with the Baptistry"*

*All numbers are based on a baptistry sized 4'x 3'x 6'. Figures have been double-checked for maximum effectiveness.

25. 232 boxes of Jell-O. Using different flavors will produce a brackish color.
26. 1,743 tablets of Alka-Seltzer wrapped in newsprint for a time-delayed effect.
27. 1 gallon of foaming bath oil.
28. 12 bottles of wet-n-clear dye (clear liquid—dries dark blue).
29. 58 Rubber Duckies (squeaking if possible).
30. 467 baking soda-powered diving mini-submarines from breakfast cereal boxes.

• • •

31. Replace the inspirational pictures in the pastor's study with portraits of Karl Marx, Lenin, and Mao.
32. On the Sunday that the most prudish elder does the pulpit Bible reading, open the Bible to Song of Solomon 7:7–8.
33. Paint the nursery black and decorate with skulls, shrunken heads, and gargoyles.

34. Use live animals for the Christmas pageant, just after the new carpet has been installed.

35. Get alone with each board member and say, "I'm really concerned about what the other board members are saying about you."

36. Change the clock that the pastor uses to run 15 minutes fast one Sunday, and then 15 minutes slow the next.

37. Change the nursery clock on an opposite schedule.

38. On a cold winter weekend, turn the thermostat way down and the baptistry heater way up. It will produce a fog bank inside the sanctuary (not available in Florida, Texas, S. California, or Arizona).

39. Bring ant farms to the church picnic.

40. Place an ad in the local yellow pages for "massage parlor" and give the church phone and address.

41. Cut small slits in the pastor's baptismal waders.

42. Rearrange the letters on the road sign to gibberish; claim to be reaching out to surrealists.

43. The old "fake severed arm under the pulpit" trick.

44. Call the church office, pretending to be a Secret Service agent arranging a presidential visit. Call back the next day canceling the trip because of suspected Communist ties among the staff

45. Replace the lighting fixtures and chandeliers with strobe lights.

46. Move the decimal point in the treasurer's report at the business meeting.

47. Change the proposed youth group budget to 50% of the church income (the kids will love you forever).

48. Have a lock-in and lose the key (then again, they may not).

49. Alter the order of worship in the bulletin to read:

    Invocation
    Rocky & Bullwinkle Show
    Same ole same ole
    Benediction

50–54 SPECIAL SECTION II:

"Rumor Mills for Fun and Prophet"

Say the following lines loudly and clearly in any setting of three or more people:

50. "Did you know the sanctuary was built on the site of a toxic waste dump?"

51. "Have you ever wondered why the pastor drives an Oldsmobile and the youth pastor still has a Pinto?"

52. "I heard the district board has put together a team to come investigate our church."

53. "The youth group sure does take a lot of mission trips to the Caribbean."

54. "I wonder what Deacon Smith was doing at Foxy Babes Dance club last night?"

• • •

55. Backward mask "The pastor is a goober head" on the church choir's cantata tapes.

56. Have the Energizer Bunny go across the stage during the sermon. (He keeps going and going and.....)

57. Replace the groom's unity candle with a trick "always light" candle at the next church wedding.

58. Switch door signs on the pastor's study and the women's restroom.

59. Put a "Sold my soul for rock and roll" bumper sticker on the organist's car.

60. Place *The Door* (or other subversive publications) inside the cover of the *Moody Monthly* in the church library.

61. Consistently ask the CE director if there are openings for Nursery workers, then find excuses for never showing up.

62. Make a fake license plate for the pastor's car that reads IAM666.

63. Send elder's name to Beer of the Month Club with church address as point of delivery.

64. When the congregation is asked for hymn requests, yell, "Louie Louie!"

65. Ketchup packets under the tires of every car in the parking lot.

66. Use the parking cones and directional arrows to make a maze—with no exit.

67. Message in the bulletin: "Beginning next week: Pastor's in-depth eight week series on the hypostatic union,

supralapsarianism, and their impact on post-modern apologetics."

68. Read the congregational prayer requests in helium voice.

69. Chaperone the 8–9 year olds on their first overnight camp out and read "The Raven" by Edgar Allen Poe.

70. Take a meat loaf topped with xxx hot sauce to the Potluck Supper.

71. Release a jar full of moths during the Missionary Slide Show.

72. Belch loudly at the end of the offertory. Look at the little old lady next to you in shock and dismay.

73. Send a letter to another church in town, challenging them to a rumble, with the words "Sprinkling is for Sissies."

74. When dedicating any new building, roll it in toilet paper the night before.

75–79 THE RETURN OF THE SPECIAL SECTION:*

*Keep a pocket camera on hand to
snap pictures of the following events.

Prints must be at least 8x10 and
plastered all over the church.

75. Pastor picking his nose.

76. Any elder/deacon giving someone "the bird" in traffic.

77. The Youth Director going to another church to steal ideas for the next youth function.

78. The Choir Director going to a Pearl Jam concert.
79. The Christian Education Director removing the helpful handouts from the curriculum packets (they do, you know they do).

• • •

80. Switch the babies in the nursery. See how long it takes the parents to find out.
81. Run the video camera for the Easter cantata and focus on someone's shoes for the entire program.
82. During a congregational business meeting refer to the board of elders as the Fascist Bourgeoisie that are oppressing the Youth.
83. Steal hymnals from different churches and use them to replace your church's hymnals, so that no two are the same.
84. Paint a "handicap only" symbol in the Pastor's reserved parking place.
85. Whenever you are asked about your Pastor refer to him as "der Führer." Nazi salute optional.
86. Put ping-pong balls in the pipes of the organ.
87. Record over the nursery copy of "Dumbo" with "Texas Chain Saw Massacre."
88. Switch the high school "sexual purity" curriculum with the 3–4 year olds' "Playing with others" curriculum.
89. Replace the pastor's sermon tapes with music from any group that has the words *Psycho, Flaming*, or *Love Gun* in its name.

90. Show up for nursery duty in Riot Gear and with a Stun Gun. (Caution: next week's worker may ask to borrow it.)
91. Announce a "kegger" party at the Pastor's house next time he goes on vacation.
92. If asked to volunteer for a committee position, reply, "Only if I can embezzle as much as ... oh you don't know about that yet."
93. The old "exploding softball" trick at the church league tournament.
94. Lace logs with chemicals to turn the next bon fire a pretty green color.
95. Get elected as a delegate to District Conference, then go to the meetings in a "Fuzzy Nose & Eyeglass" set.
96. Take sulfuric acid to the next car wash.
97. Use a flame thrower as an object lesson for Sunday school.
98. Release a couple dozen crickets in the church offices.
99. Welcome visitors to the church with the phrase "Thank you for coming. Robes are over there, sign over all your assets, and the head shaving is free."
100. Hang a sign on the front door that reads "$100 minimum tithe. All others will be shot."
101. Stand up and tell the truth about a life changed by Christ. Nothing irritates the dead like seeing the living enjoy life.

ABOUT THE AUTHOR

Donald T. Williams (BA Taylor University, M.Div. Trinity Evangelical Divinity School, PhD University of Georgia) is Professor Emeritus of Humanities at Toccoa Falls College in the hills of northeast Georgia. He is a past president of the International Society of Christian Apologetics and an ordained minister in the Evangelical Free Church of America. He has spent several summers training national pastors in places like Uganda, Kenya, and India for Church Planting International. A dual citizen of Narnia and Middle-earth, he is a border dweller, permanently camped out on the borders between serious scholarship and pastoral ministry, theology and culture, poetry and apologetics. He is the author of many articles, poems, and reviews in various journals and of sixteen other books, including *Credo: Meditations on the Nicene Creed, 2nd ed.* (Middletown, RI: 2025).